Appalachian Gothic Tales

by
Jean Battlo

1997
McClain Printing Company
212 Main Street
Parsons, West Virginia 26287

International Standard Book Number 0-87012-577-X
Library of Congress Catalog Card Number 97-093246
Printed in the United States of America
Copyright © 1997 by Jean Battlo
Kimball, West Virginia 24853
All Rights Reserved

The Apple People of Johnnycake Mountain

"Man is a political animal," said Aristotle, telling one of the greatest lies in human history. For every man has more in common with the hills, or the stars, than with other men.
----Colin Wilson: The Mind Parasites

If you had asked anyone on Johnnycake Mountain if there were anything strange or a little odd about the Applbys who had the orchard over on Johnnycake Mountain, anyone and everyone would have told you, "No, not a thing strange about those folks." And, everyone would have added, "The Applbys grew the best, the tastiest, the appleiest apples in the whole of the Cumberland and Appalachian mountain ranges."

Oh, sure, Ned and Cindy Applby didn't come down to town. No, nor were they ones for visiting nor joining a regular Baptist church like everyone else. Truth to tell, they weren't much for any sort of involvement with people, but no one paid that much never mind. Most of the people in the regions where the Applbys grew apples either lived on mountains or had once lived there; they were generally of original British stock and kept pretty much to themselves.

The average family along the ridge, even shoving into the Twenty-First Century, still tended to be larger than those of mainstream America and were extended and close-knit. Fact of the matter was most of them saw fit to stay within their own kind for any social purposes. As much as possible they even limited their young's adventuresomeness to going to school, and not encouraging that all that much. So, through a couple of centuries, the Collinses, Jacksons, Lesters, the Blankenships, Mullinses and Lockharts never noticed anything peculiar about the Applbys.

In fact, everyone liked the Applbys. Liked them as much as

they did any family; knew very little about their personal lives, or even if they had any. The one thing certain everyone knew about Applbys was apples, and that each autumn in anyone's memory, the eldest son of the Applby clan would come into town, set up at Farmers' Market for a month or so, sell apples and cider, then, silent as an apple tree, go back up the mountain. Always, and only, the eldest son, and he would not be seen again until spring when he came down for seed.

Oh, yeah, those Applbys were rooted in those mountains, their land running from Johnnycake Mountain all the way east to Estep Ridge. That was all anyone outside the family knew.

But within the Applby clan, they knew.

The Applby roots on Johnnycake Mountain could be traced back over two centuries to when old Zechariah Bennoble Applby reached into the far reaches of what was then the western part of the colony of Virginia. Family rumor was that old Zechariah may have sown some other Applbys on his trek west from Williamsburg; but family fact was recorded in the Applby Bible when Zechariah, on June 8, 1797, "took to wife" one Carella SueBelle Milem. It seems that old Zech immediately planted apple trees and the Applbys were set.

The Bible records the births of Zechariah and Carella's children: Thomas, born Jan. 8, 1798; Sara, born Aug. 11, 1799; Abraham, born Oct. 4, 1801; Benjamin, born July 4, 1803, and on through four more sons and three daughters that kept coming until apparently Carella's womb shut down in 1815. Then, the Bible goes on to list the marriages and the next generation of births and the next, etc. Odd thing, the Bible does not list the deaths. Maybe the Applbys did not like to record sadness, but it was a singular thing.

According to stories Ned told his son, Bobby, Zechariah had told his son that apples had been part of family legend since the original Anglo-Saxon ancestry had had orchards in far England, from where Zechariah claimed to have brought first seeds. Some theories were that the family name had derived from those same apple orchards. From time to time, in their history, some had put forth the tale that their origins and orchards went back even farther than the British Isles. Tobias Applby, born in 1872, claimed that he had an old family book, kept private except for the eldest son of the eldest son, etc., and that that book gave evidence of the family's mystic beginnings in the Mediterranean.

Tobias had noted some work that meant nothing to others at the time, but included things like Pythagoras, pyramids, Etruscans, Eleusis and mysteries. But the modern American Applbys did not seem to care much for the words.

Ned Applby admitted to his son that he really didn't know any of those words, except mystery and pyramids. Ned allowed how he had memorized the words along with some other poem-like or recipe-like words because the head of the family always did that, and he didn't know but what he might need them. Ned said he didn't trouble his head about them; if you needed to know the origins of orchards and how to act to please the Creator, Ned felt you could pretty much trust Genesis.

They were just simple apple farmers. Ned would laugh when someone said that they had apple juice in their veins instead of blood. And it seemed that in all their family history, not one who was born of the "juice" didn't have a love for the gnarled bent twisting arms of the tree limbs; for the sweet scented pink-white blossomings of spring, right through the first taut tart sour-sweet taste of the fruit on all their autumn evenings.

So, to the whole county and neighboring ones alike, the Applbys were just ordinary people who had great orchards of delicious apples, spotless, yet without any evidence of worms, nor any possibility of the use of sprays anywhere on them. That's all. That's what everyone said, everyone except Colt Jenkins.

Colt Jenkins said it looked real funny to him that there weren't any Applbys moving off the mountain like everybody else in McDowell County, moving over to Jolo or Stringtown, Long Pole, and even Hazard, Kentucky. After coal failed, the Lesters and the Blankenships, Lockharts and Mullinses, everyone left; but no Applby was ever known to leave Johnnycake Mountain.

And that's another thing that got to Colt; where did they get their husbands and wives; seemed a lot like when Adam and Eve's kids were getting their spouses East of Eden. But where did the Applbys get their's; somebody tell Colt that! But, Colt imbibed some. In a little more than apple cider, so when he said all his sayings, no one paid him any never mind. Truth to tell, people were just as happy to get shed of Colt as to listen to him.

Excepting Jessie Jenkins. Jessie was married to Colt, so she had no choice but to listen to all the nonsense, which was what Jessie told Colt -- all nonsense! She told Colt that the younger Applbys had probably gone off the way most young do after graduating, and were probably planting apples in California or North Carolina by now. Well, what about their elders! Them that come before Ned and Cindy, Colt would like to know. Maybe California, Jessie reasoned, maybe North Carolina or maybe just died off.

Well, now there you have it, that is another thing, Colt would be slurring and by this point in the conversation, "Nother thing I don't get is how come we never have been to an Applby wake! You explain that to me, no, nor a funeral and how come there isn't any Applbys over at GreenLawn Cemetery!" Although Colt might be standing and shouting, "How come?", at her, Jessie would walk off, but truth to tell, it was a thought that got hung in her mind.

Sometimes, when Jessie wasn't too mad to talk more, she'd advise Colt how a lot of mountain people buried their own on the mountainsides; had their own private family plots, and Jessie figured the Applbys to do just that. Figured they didn't like all that public sitting and wailing, nor the preaching about how God wanted another flower for his bouquet.

Yeah, well, Colt would rare up anew, well how come in over his seventy years living at the foot of that mountain he hadn't never ever even heard tell of one of them Applbys so much as dying. But Jessie's patience would be wore and she would leave Colt alone on the porch steps with his homemade plum wine and his early autumn evening thoughts until he was unconscious again.

That continued for years and years and years until time got around to the 1960s, and Bobby Applby got killed over in Asia. That changed everything. For some autumns after that Ned and Cindy would come to the market themselves, what with their oldest boys killed and God alone knowing where their other children were. There had to be others. Probably grandchildren, but this was something the eldest did, and the guess was that Ned felt that the torch had been passed back to him.

Here he would come down in that '37 pickup Ford that would have been dead had another man besides Ned owned it. No one could recall such a sight. Ned had not come down to town himself since he was a young man. As soon as Bobby was able he took up the task. And now, here was Ned, had to be pushing eighty and bringing down the apples himself.

Later, when talk finally did commence, there were those who had questions aplenty, but it was too late for answers. All that Sheriff Ballard Hicks could get was a smattering of statements from the last person known to have talked to the old couple.

Of course, Colt Jenkins came forward to tell the sheriff what he thought: That the Applbys were strange folk, that he'd never been to one of their wakes, which he thought was real, real, real peculiar, and besides, he thought there was something that went on with those people on that mountain that never went on with anyone anywheres else. That's what Colt thought, though he couldn't put his finger on just what it was went on, but nothing would surprise him because they were sure the appleliest people. In fact, it seemed like their whole heart and very souls were apples. He did not know anyone who did know of anything an Applby said or did that was not apples.

"No one did," Sheriff Hicks said softly. He excused himself and went on through the county looking for clues to this disappearance. Because, truth to tell, the old couple were gone -- just gone. No one ever saw them leave; no one saw them even come off the mountain, but they were gone. When Ned and Cindy didn't come down that fall, Hicks went to check on them but he could not find hide nor hair of them.

Hicks counted himself lucky to have found a sober voice in Josh Jim Rollins who owned Rollins Grain and Grocery. Josh Jim could not so much tell what he had seen as what he had not seen. He had not seen Old Ned come down for seed last spring. No, nor had he come down this autumn when he was due.

So, word came plummeting down the mountain; Josh Jim Rollins had been the last person to see Old Ned and Cindy in his store the autumn prior. Colt put it like this, "Josh Jim was the last to see Old Ned and Cindy alive." But no one was of a humor to pay Colt any mind. People around were concerned enough, never you mind about that, but still and all, they didn't want to pry, so everyone just waited winter.

With the first slush of spring thaw, Ballard Hicks felt bound to return to have a look-see around the house and orchard. When he got there all he found was rich loamy earth, strong healthy trees and the beginnings of buds about to burst the boughs with bloom.

And a deserted farmhouse.

Hicks searched the whole house, all the rooms, closets, etc. Nothing. When he arrived, the front door was wide opened, though there was no evidence of human life within. On the other hand, neither was there any evidence of harm or violence, no disorder, nothing overturned. It was simply as if the Applbys had walked right out the front door, leaving it open for a breeze to enter while they took an evening walk among the apple blossoms.

Ballard Hicks returned to the kitchen as if fully expecting to find Ned and Cindy sitting there waiting with a cup of cider in their hand. Expected Ned to be as friendly as Josh Jim said he'd been that last day, wishing Josh Jim a warm winter, mentioning the price of apples, handling his crates as if he held gold, never mentioning Bobby, but saying people should eat more apples; talking like poetry about apples being God's gift, and then, going out of the door, saying, "Well, Josh Jim, I guess that's it."

When Colt heard that he started to speculate but...

Everyone walked off.

One other thing Josh Jim said, said Ned looked very, very old, bent, sort of gnarled. Said his skin seemed unusually brown, which Josh Jim just took to show the old man was doing all the outdoor work himself that summer. Ha, Josh Jim said he said to himself as he watched the old man shuffle to his pickup, he looks like an old tree himself.

But Hicks couldn't let it alone. He went back up and took some deputies with him. They went over the place with a fine tooth comb: nothing. Went through barns and the shed -- nothing. No sign of foul, or fair play; just a whole big bushel of nothing.

Finally, as a last resort, not for a moment influenced by Colt's assurance that somebody's gone up and killed those fine old people and buried them in the orchard amongst their trees; Hicks and his deputies scoured the orchard inch by inch, foot by foot, tree by tree.

Nothing.

Then just as they were leaving, young Preston Bailey said, "Look there; there's two little saplings just starting to bud." He bent to them, "Fine looking. I ought to dig them up and take them for Betty Sue to plant."

"No." Ballard said quickly, looking at the saplings, knowing the case was closed, "Leave them alone. They're right where they're supposed to be."

In the Eye of George Mahotep

I

When George Mahotep was found dead in his solitary mountain cabin in May of 1950, the little town of Campbell, West Virginia assumed murder. In large part because the ax that had split his skull all but floated in the pool of blood beside his body; a singular fact which set the abnormally safe small Appalachian town abuzz with rumor and speculation for all a summer long.

George Mahotep had first arrived, seemingly from nowhere, to the isolated mountain town in 1939. Though he spoke little English, he was able to communicate to townspeople that he could do any and all types of home and garden work. Proving to be an exceptional handy man, Mahotep was soon being hired for everything from cobbling shoes to mending roofs. Though he worked in silence, presumably from ignorance of the language, his friendly demeanor made him more welcome than strangers generally were in town. In a phrase, as Howie Tolliver, proprietor of the town's Esso station put it, "Everyone likes George."

Maybe, Rhoda Cantrell, the beauty operator at Turn a Curl rebutted, but that all-the-time-silent-smile on his face just might mask some terrible secret. And, naturally Rhoda's dire prophetic assumptions had taken on hair when, three months after his first arrival, George Mahotep disappeared.

The more benign town theorists held that George had simply gone off to his own county, wherever in the world that might be, to help stop Hitler. "Humph!", said, Rhoda and her ilk. But the benign neighbors won the day when, in the summer of 1945, without fanfare or the accompanying kudos of other local heroes, George Mahotep returned to Campbell. He neither confirmed nor denied where he had been during the time he was away, but it was evident that he meant to stay in the obscure town permanently.

The mountain land surrounding Campbell, West Virginia, was owned by either coal or railroad companies which didn't much want it unless it was being stripped. When not in use, the companies made it available for a nominal fee. George leased a quarter-acre from the Pendleton Coal Company near the foot of Belcher Mountain, just a half-hill up from Carswell Hollow. Mahotep built his one-room Thoreauvian cabin, moved in, planted his garden, and seemed as content as a character in a mountain novel of another, less bellicose era.

So successful was he at odd jobs that the McDowell County Board of Education hired George as janitor for Campbell Elementary. From that point on, George's life appeared to be pure delight. Whatever truth was his past, whatever stories, or lives and loves it contained and lost, George had an almost awesome love for children; and in the 1950s, that was all right. Children, in turn, innocent and tolerant, seemed to think they discovered Santa Claus' brother, a truly wonderman, in George Mahotep.

George was the sort of old man to tuck away in one's memory forever; to be recalled as you grew older, as near legend. He wore a scruffy baggy old black jacket from the "old country", which no one had ever been able to identify, thus, George was mystery. He had none of the long lists of rules and codes of the also legendary "adults", so he gave self-esteem and a sense of acceptance. But perhaps best of all were the great bulges on his side pockets which were kept crammed full of candies, given to any child for the asking.

If a child fell on the playground, or came to any harm, they ran to George. If a parent could not find a tardy child, they checked the school halls for Old George. If a child's feelings were hurt by a teacher or student, George Mahotep was the answer. Old George would heal the wound, salve the broken heart or feeling.

Adults marveled because he still did not seem to know a word of English, yet there was no barrier between him and the children. GraceEllen Wilcox claimed that there was a communication between George and the children, not unlike essences contained in math; but Miss Wilcox was the only one in Campbell who talked like that and no one knew what she meant.

Whatever form that communication took, it was from the children that the adults learned that George had been born in the land of Egypt. Robby Johnson, the top geography student in fourth grade said he had known it all along because he had figured it from George's last name. But Sally Blankenship said, if Robby knew so much how come he hadn't told, huh? Anyway! Robby went on, there was not a single other person in McDowell County, maybe not in the whole entire state of West Virginia that came from Egypt. George was making Campbell famous. And that wasn't even the half of it, if you could credit anything Robby Johnson said, he said that the word gypsy came from Egypt, so what did they bring to Campbell, huh?

And like the whipped cream and cherry on top of the sundaes you got at Kopper's Drug Store, George had a necklace that he showed the children. No one in Campbell, West Vir-

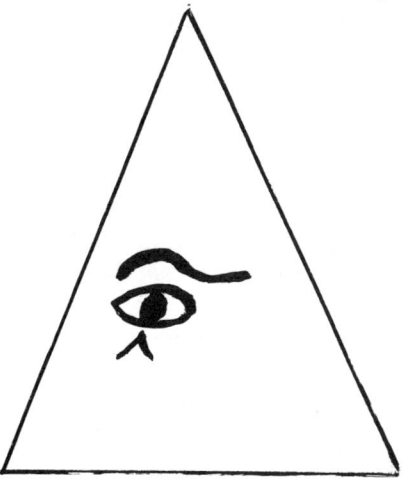

ginia in 1950 had ever seen anything like it. It looked like this:

The children did a great deal of speculating about that necklace. Jessie Collins thought they should just up and ask George what it was, but Betty Sue Lester said they shouldn't do that, that might hurt his feelings and George would never hurt their feelings. Brandon York thought it might be some Catholic thing 'cause Catholics had a lot of things like that, but Teresa Roschella got all huffy and said it was NOT a Catholic thing! Finally, retard Jere Joe Robert went right up and said, "George's what that?"

All the children shuddered as one, but George did not get angry as adults usually did when you asked them something. Instead, George said nothing, simply bowed his head so the kids

11

knew it was about God.

But now George was dead.

All the children were distraught. Some so much so that their parents kept them home from school.

There was a great to-do, but nothing really to do about the murder. The school officials urged the investigation and it was all done as thoroughly as possible but nothing was ever discovered.

It had not been the type of murder that fit any of the classic categories of murder mysteries. George had no known enemies; he seemed to be a truly good man.

He had no possessions in his cabin which was a well-known fact in the whole county, so that ruled out local offenders. Besides, no one could seriously believe that anyone in or around Campbell could commit a crime anyway.

On the other hand, if anyone had come to his cabin unexpectedly and wanted something, George would have given it to them. But that very idea could be ruled out by the fact that no one would go into the mountains so deep as where George had built his cabin. So, there was simply no motive known in the annals of criminal studies for someone to murder George Mahotep.

Nonetheless, because of the esteem in which he was held, the authorities continued the investigation for some time. Officer Jim Franklin said they owed that to their young. But all of the officers were obviously baffled and it was generally understood that there was no real hope of finding the murderer.

Strangers never made their way into this area of Appalachia, and if they had, they would have been noted as strangers and that fact would have flown around town in four seconds. There were some, including Rhoda Cantrell, who thought there might be someone from George's "shady" past that finally found him and did the deed. That idea grew hair on its chest because the ax that had halved George's skull, and as we later learned, had hacked the body into various parts, lay right beside the body making it obvious that the culprit had no fear of detection.

What was to become the most famous ax in southern West Virginia history was saturated with globs of blood. No fingerprints were ever found.

Cities had numerous unsolved murders Sheriff Hicks noted, but this was the strangest of things. Because, to his recollection, Campbell had never so much as had a single murder; let alone an unsolved murder. So, after two years, the case was closed. And in all that time there had never been one official word or hint that anyone could call a "clue" to the killing of George Mahotep.

II

Williamsburg, Virginia; autumn, 1996.
The empty rocking chair was rocking.
As it had done last evening. And as it had done one evening in August. But Nita Baker, B.S., Ph.D. William and Mary, 1978 knew that an empty chair could not be rocking.
Still, the chair rocked, back and forth, back and forth.
Nita looked straight at the chair, lit a cigarette and sat on the couch opposite and for some moments simply stared at the rocking chair. She began a series of calculations: 1) there could be some imperceptible breeze entering the room, or 2) it could be some sort of nervous twitching, or some odd floating effect with her eyes caused by the last seventy-two, non-stop hours in the lab without food or rest, or 3) a set of hallucinogenic mental quirks brought on by #2, plus the decanter of martinis to relax her, and or, simply too much Edgar Allan Poe and Hitchcock as a child.
A twitch of a smile crossed Nita's lips at the thought. She could not now believe that even as a child she had read such tripe. However, it did not seem probable that her childhood fears could cause the current mental havoc that made the impossible appear possible. Yet, perhaps some childhood fallacy of conceptualization was reoccurring in her psyche; perhaps even a flashback experience from her experimentation with LSD and other hallucinogenic drugs was the basis for what she perceived herself as experiencing at this moment.
What Dr. Nita Baker was absolutely certain of was that there was no spirit, ghost, apparition or alleged poltergeist operative.
And yet, as Nita sipped her martini, that empty chair was rocking.
Angered by anything she couldn't explain Nita got up and went to her bed and began to pile pillows behind her back. She

lit another cigarette off of the first one; put that one out. She got up and turned on all the lights in the house so that she could focus fully, stare at that rocking chair in the lucidity of artificial light until it conformed with reality as Nita Baker understood reality. She was not some sniffling foolish little feminine creature shuddering at Halloweens 14, 18, or 30-something, however many they had made.

Nita was widely awake, and that made her all the more angry because her mind and body told her how urgently she needed sleep if she was going to sit through the next night with her specimens. Yet here she sat, Nita Baker, BS, MA, Ph.D. staying awake, imagining that an empty chair was rocking. Nita took a deep drag on the cigarette, drank her martini and said aloud in a calm resonating reasonable if somewhat irritated voice, "That chair is not rocking."

The chair rocked. Gently. Purposively.

III

The grisly rat scurried across the room.

The room was as silent as a space in Ur might have been a million years ago but for the soft furry scurry of the gaunt gray creature.

In the entombment of the silent room, that rat was the last of three dozen which were slowly being starved to death as part of the experiment. Now the tiny creature slumped to the floor, nearly dead, precisely as the huge metal doors swooshed open and two white clad people entered.

"Oh, look over there," the young doctor said, "---in the corner, Brad Pitt is all pooped out."

Dr. Baker, who did not approve of naming the mice for actors, said laconically, "Check his pulse and heartbeat quickly."

"Ok, Brad, roll up your shirtsleeves."

Nita spoke more firmly, "Mr. Hackett, you have to hurry. Every second counts when studying the death process. If he goes into a coma before we check the rates, I'll be losing valuable data."

"I know. Last minutes reactions and all that. Let's go, Brad."

Nita hated working with undergraduates; they were all so frivolous. "Mr. Hackett, if you ever again refer to one of the specimens by a private nomenclatures in my presence, I'll have you dismissed from this project."

"Private nomen...", the young man didn't complete the phrase; big bitch Baker was common (and all assumed, never carnal-) knowledge among her assistants. Hackett began checking the mouse.

"And our relationship will go better if you refrain from responding to me at all. Your type foolishness has impeded significant scientific advancement ever since the undergraduate programs began."

"Were you born with your degrees?"

"You are skating on the thinnest of ices. Now this ...", Nita pointed to the mouse, "is Specimen #34."

"Dr. Baker I was only..."

"You were only being personal. Emotional. 'Cute', if you will. And as usual, failing to get your work done properly. I will not allow anyone..."

"Whoa! Whoa whoa, I just..." Hackett stopped his defense and spoke with near sadness, "He's dead. Ah, Brad."

"Good." Nita opened the laptop computer she was carrying and made notes, "That is almost precisely on the minute of my prediction that he would die."

"That's great for you."

Nita added, "Another day of life would have meant an error in my projected estimation..."

"God forbid."

Nita did hear that and turned on Hackett with fury, but he went on, "I know it's only a mouse, but talking about life as a calculation..."

"You know, Hackett, I think you should leave science for the priesthood. I've thought that all along. Emotion can be destructive and when it comes at the cost of information, it's anathema. I thought I had made that clear."

"But Dr. Baker, I was only commenting on the fact that when you spend day after day with any living thing, it seems to develop a persona of sorts. I didn't meant that I was in love with this mouse."

"Let me make something clear, Hackett, in case I've misled you. I'm not one of those professors who consider assistants friends. I think of you as just that, some persona placed at my disposal to assist and do exactly what I need done."

"That is entirely clear, Dr. Baker."

"Good. Further, if I am not on the board that examines your thesis, be sure that I will be asked to be placed on it. I have reservations about your getting a degree from my institution."

"Your institution?"

"Don't doubt it. Are you even aware of the international attention given my projects here."

"I do know how important your work is. Do you know that I especially asked to be placed with you. In a world with a dwindling food supply, these studies in starvation..."

"Could in time, save lives! Then act like you understand! But if you came on just because you thought this was simply some humanitarian study about food supplies, you are gravely mistaken. My dear fool, I've been studying the death-process all my life. This starvation study is just one of many which I'm using because of the funding. I'm not interested in the food programs, Hackett. I'm interested in the results of the process of dying this way. I simply want to find out how long, if and what effects various deprivations have on the living organism."

"But beyond that, didn't you hope..."

"Beyond that, in terms of my research, nothing. If you intend to save the world, you need another project director." Then Nita closed the laptop and hurried from the room before Hackett could comment.

IV

"Ah, that feels good." Like a lot of people who live alone, Nita did her thinking aloud, often holding complete two-party conversations with herself. Now she verbalizd the good feeling as she sank into the hot waters and oils of her bath. She luxuriated in the feeling for some moments, closing her eyes and ears so that she could concentrate all her senses and self to the feel of the fluids inundating her body. It was so soothing that she almost fell asleep.

Abruptly, Nita sat bolt upright in the tub just as her head was about to go under water. That's when she saw it.

Again. Or sensed it; just an instantaneous flutter of light there in the corner of her eye. "Damn, not something else." Nita rubbed her eyes, "First an empty rocking chair and now this?"

But what was "this"? Once more Dr. Baker put her rationalizing expertise into operation; "This", was probably fatigue from the long hours of work and the annoying boy they gave her to work with. Perhaps wind had come in the window in the hallway and the draft had caused the curtain to flutter, and of course, there was always that common optical trick of floaters, "Ahhhhhhh," Nita screamed and leaped out of the tub.

Trying to think of the comical side of it, Nita stood in the middle of the floor, naked and shivering. But she was frightened, too frightened to even reach for a towel. Though she knew perfectly well that such phenomenon could not occur, she did clearly see, for a micro-second, an elongated steel object raised in the air just to the left of her head.

Out of thin air; something out of nothing; effect without a cause.

Nita let the thought slowly seep into her consciousness, held it a moment, then once more tried to dismiss it, "No, no, I saw no such thing."

She grabbed the towel and tied it around her, once more confirming that her nerves were raw; the thought of Hackett made them more raw, and as soon as she completed this next series of tests, she must take some time off. As Nita started down the hallway to her bedroom, she almost flipped the hall lights on, but then mocked herself for being so silly. She went to the bedroom without further incidence.

See, silly old girl, Nita laughed, you're slipping just when you cannot afford to do so. Not now. The whole world is about to be at your feet; you're on top of it, possible Nobel growing more probable each day. There's more and more attention given the project and lots of good press from people who see what they want to see in it; enough to insure grants to your heart's content for lots of years. Enough veiled projects so that you can study until you know more about death than any living person ever has known.

"Oh, no." Nita barely sighed the gasp because she heard the sound even before the lights were on in her room. The soft crunch of sound on her oaken floors, the creak of wood on wood; Nita flipped the lights on so that she could stare and there in the glare of the lightened room, the chair rocked.

Gently, back and forth and back and forth, gently, though it seemed vicious. Gradually, it became vicious, real as if it had a consciousness of its own and the rocking grew more and more furious as if a strong angry man was being forced to sit in the chair and was taking his anger out in the thrust of wild rocking.

Nita would not scream again; she just whispered, "No." Then she started across the room repeating, "No, no, no, you are not going to do this to me. Not now. Not after all these years; nothing is happening here." Mentally, she began to address the chair itself: "You are an inanimate object. What appears to be your rocking can be explained by calm cold logic if I can maintain that. This is not really happening; I only perceive it to be happening for some reason. For some reason, I may even be the cause of this deluded perception."

Nita walked straight over to the rocking chair to observe it more closely. The closer she got, the more furious the rocking became until, when she was standing beside it, its swift movement was so strong it actually fanned her body.

Determined to best every situation, Nita forced herself to reach out to the chair to stop it. With another more muffled scream, she pulled her hand away only to see an immediate blistering swell begin in the palm of her right hand where she had touched the chair. At first, so horrified by the experience itself, Nita did not detect the form the wound was taking. Then, her horror gave way to pain and anger, "We'll, see," she said, though her voice lacked some of its usual timbre.

V

The weeks that followed seemed to Nita to be the life of someone else other than herself. The experiences which she was, from time to time, forced to admit seemed to be occurring to her, had to be other than hers. In order to ignore, and in part, as an aid in their denial, Nita worked even longer hours in the lab, the one place where no "manifestation" ever happened to her. "Manifestation" was the term she had finally settled on after considering several others suitable to use until she overcame the silly situation.

Yet, though nothing untoward ever occurred in the lab, it did everywhere else; continuously, on the ceiling above her bed at night; across the street from her bed at night; across the street from her office, and one clear day, in the sky, hovering over the college playing field.

Living alone with the situation for over a month, Nita decided, against her better judgment, that she should maybe consider trusting in someone else's intellect. What she knew of Angus Johnson, noted scion of the psychology department did not impress her, but if she was going to suffer any of those insufferable academes, it would most definitely have to be Angus.

Actually, Nita had always thought Angus stupid and it only took fifteen minutes with him professionally to confirm the thought. Of the rocking chair, which was as much as Nita had confided, keeping her fists clinched throughout the confession, Angus had said nothing she found meritorious. Nita felt she knew his field almost as well as he. She updated her own reading in his field which obviously he did not and thus he was at variance with many of her conclusions. What he did have to say was elementary, ideas which she had developed and dismissed from the first instant of incident.

Angus Johnson was a waste. Nita left his office hurriedly, deciding that 1) she must accept the fact that she had somehow become emotionally at risk and the result was that she was temporarily intellectually impaired so that for the first time in her life, she must question her perception, and 2) she must resist the apparition, face and control it, keeping in mind that it only appeared to be there; that her own mind was creating the situation for some reason, but it had no veritable reality. It was almost that very moment that the shape again formed, this time in the palm of her left hand.

VI

Nita could no longer eat or sleep.
Day by day she grew weaker and weaker.
She was awarded the Nobel Prize but could not attend.
She was awarded the grant to begin her new project, working with terminal patients, and she would do it, she determined.
Nita raised her hand as if to swear to herself that she would begin the new project but when her hand was raised, she saw it. It was fully developed now; complete.

VII

When Nita parked the car in front of the building, she looked up and down the dark deserted street furtively, to be certain no one from the campus would see her entering the strange house. Secure that no one was near, Nita stealthily got out of the car and ran to the door as quickly as her weakened condition allowed. Before she could knock, just as she was raising her gloved hand, the door opened.

Nita was startled by the appearance of the very ordinary man who answered the door. Her shock was so obvious that the man laughed outright. "You expected horns and a tail, no doubt?"

He lifted his hand to stop her, "Don't apologize. The world is full of misconceptions. I'm sure you have had many in your own work, Dr. Baker."

Without responding, Nita followed him into his study and sat where he indicated, not allowing herself to look about at the unusual paraphenalia in the room. She did not want him to mistake her visit as an interest in his "faith". Regardless of her intention not to do so, Nita began commandingly, "I don't want to insult you, but I must make this absolutely clear from the beginning..."

"You do not believe in the occult, the supernational or anything remotely associated with the same."

"I suppose this means you are telepathic." Nita pulled out a cigarette as he laughed again, and without asking permission, told him, "I have to smoke."

As she lit the cigarette and began smoking, he told her, "Dr. Baker, I don't want to insult you either, but your beliefs or lack of them are of no interest to me whatsoever. Nor are you, to be terribly honest. So don't undermind us both by assuming that role of academic royalty."

Nita had to contain her growing anger. He was a last resort so she had to try to sustain this interview. He was laying his cards on the table openly, "Your phone call sounded desperate. You asked for my help. It is part of my belief system to help when I can. You will, without doubt, be disarmed to think there are people in the world that would like to do good, but I know those numbers to be legion."

Nita couldn't bare it. She snuffed out the cigarette, "I am

not here to discuss theology or ethics."

"You are but you don't know it. But do get to the point so that we can bother each other as little as possible."

For some inexplicable reason, Nita did feel a slight remorse, "I'm sorry. I don't mean to be so blunt."

"Don't apologize. We are who we are, and where we are supposed to be at this moment."

Once more, Nita doubted she was going to be able to go through with this meeting, "If you mean to suggest reincarnation, I do not..."

"I'm sure you don't believe in it either. Now, to the point. What made you decide to come to me at all?"

"I was driving by one day and --- I saw your --- icon, I guess you'd call it. What is your group?"

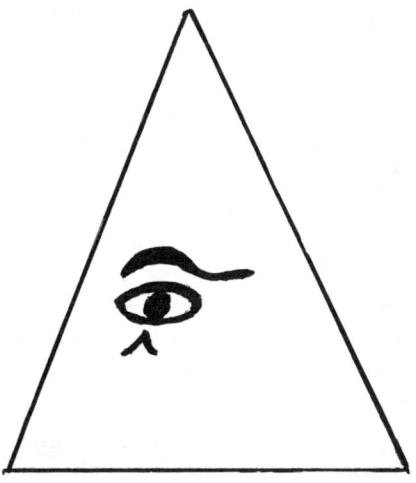

"That annoys me. I know that you know my studies relate to Ahura Mazda, Dr. Baker. With your erudite education, I doubt you missed much and I..."

"Look at this!" Nita jerked off the glove and thrust her hand at him. The master only barely suppressed a gasp, "Did you...how have you had that imprinted?"

"Now are you pretending ignorance? You know this is not imprinted. It's imbedded, beneath the skin. Look at it!" On Nita's hand was the completed sign:

"What is it?" Nita asked.

The master swallowed, "You know what it is."

"Say it, please." Her voice was desperate, "Please."

His voice was controlled, but it was apparently with effort, "Some say, the Eye of Osiris. More correctly, though the two gods are often merged into one, it is the Eye of Horus." He spoke with haste, wanting her to leave, "I'm certain that with your scholarship, you're familiar with the societies and cultures and faiths that claim it."

"The Egpytian theogony."

"Yes."

"Tell me. I don't know anything but the names. I gather that it's a polytheistic religion. Then, what is the area of their power? I mean, doesn't each god have a jurisdiction, some realm that they reign in?"

The master was studying Nita's face. More calmed now he told her, "Osiris is The Good, and he judges. Horus is even more the god of absolute justice, even revenge. Or more precisely, retribution."

"This is ridiculous." Nita got up and began to pace, "It's utter nonsense. I can't believe I came here."

"Then by all means, leave."

"You listen, I don't for a minute believe any of this."

"Believe any of what. I've not suggested any belief system to you. You asked a question. I answered it very simply."

"Well, I just want to make clear that all I'm after is information, so don't try to con me." Nita got her handbag as if to leave, "I am going. No, just one thing more, let me tell you one thing..." Speaking irrationally, Nita was flaying her hands and thus was once again confronted with the image; unnerved, she immediately changed her tactics, "Suppose I accepted some of this, I know you aren't really making any judgements, but say I was a student of Ahura Mazda, I mean, why is this stigmata on my hand? What have I done?"

"Dr. Baker, you must try to calm yourself."

"You don't understand!" Like a watershed, the dams of Nita's emotions seemed to break through, "For the first time in my life, I am almost happy. That has never been true. Not in my childhood, no, especially not in my childhood. So why, what is persecuting me?"

The master's eye pierced Nita, and yet was compassionate, "Only you can answer that, Dr. Baker."

"To hell with you!" Nita left the room so rapidly that she knocked over the statuette of Isis.

VIII

"All right, all right, all right!" Nita stayed rocking in the rocking chair, chanting the litany, "All right, all right, all right."

IX

The ambulance left with the broken body of Nita Baker. Inspector Rondo looked up to her apartment, "Cheez, seventeen stories."

"Yeah. If people are going to all the time be killing themselves, maybe this county ought to promote that French book on suicides so they could do it a little nicer," Police Chief Fields said.

"Lady was a Nobel Prize winner, you know that."

"Well, she splattered like she was one of us ordinary people."

"Chief, you have the sensitivities of a serial killer."

"I know. But you have to work on distance." He sighed and held the piece of paper toward Rondo, "Did you see this?"

"Yeah. No matter how much you see, it stays a little incredible."

"Yeah." The chief read the note again,

I have been a consummate scientist all my life, "from childhood's hour," in fact. My earliest memories are of becoming enthralled with the idea of death, and I began at a very early age to investigate the subject. While still in grade school, I began my studies, dissecting insects, frogs, and birds, etc. Naturally, unfortunately, I had to kill them in order to study the death process. As unsavory as the act of killing was for a child, I felt from the very first that the end result of what I would one day discover, warranted, no, mandated, that I pursue the work. I had no doubt whatsoever that my work, continued as an adult, would eventuate in physical immortality for those who would wish it.

I was convinced, that just as a machine can be repaired

indefinitely by the knowing mechanic, just so, the body, that magnificent machine, can also be repaired indefinitely. The key was to be found in the death process.

Though a child, I soon realized that if my end results were to be relative to the human machine, that no matter how many bugs, insects, frogs or birds I killed and watched through the process, I must in fact, look to the source itself: human life.

The realization grew until it became my one subjective imperative; I had to observe a human death. I also assessed, that as a perfect little "model" ten-year-old, gifted, and a teacher's pet, I could expect to perform my experiment without impediment, and assuredly without suspicion.

There lived in my town a useless, unproductive odd old man named George – – –

μὐστηζ

The One

Like some gray ghost he moved through the Appalachian woods as the autumn night let its first graying fog drift through the thick tall pines. At times the fog brewed so thick that the full moon completely disappeared. But he had no time nor thought for moons this night. In and out of the trees, weaving through their spaces, in and out of wooded clumps, through tanglewood aperatures and mossy crevices, small crawling beasts scurried with soft hurried sounds, though these, too, he could not notice.

Viewed from a distance, he might seem, as he roved between old oaks and elms to be some medieval monk in some far time ago. As indeed he had once been, in those times, out then, too, through other curious forests on what then was thought to be omnious occult business. He smiled at the memory. That had been a pleasant time for him; a pleasant place. But now, as the Twenty-First Century loped into the annals of history, They had thought it best to place him in this obscure hermit's hut in the most remote mountains of what the Moderns called West Virginia. Odd, he mused, the varying names and words in the languages of time.

Then, he sighed, for They had concluded that these Moderns might be about to turn history's pages back to that maimed Middle Period. He shuddered, hoping it would not come to the Necessity. Though he feared it must.

Soon, these proud Moderns would have to be on their knees again, begging, pleading and trembling as They had often been forced to reduce them, even prior to the time of the cold stone walls, the odd assortment of their saints and icons. Not so odd, if they could understand the ultimate truths in symbolism, that cross. It was sad though, when they could now create those conditions which would make human life the happiest of all times, that there were those among them still unleashing the dogs of hate and war. Yet, foolish though he was, Infinity forgive him, he still loved these silly creatures, and it saddened him to fool them, again.

At the edge of forest, near a place they called Carswell Hollow where there had once been a coal mine, near a clearing, he stood a long time gazing at the occasional moon, arguing with himself. After all, They had avoided the use of Method for nearly seven hundred years now. He hated to revert back to it; he had always been the one to oppose the use of Method anyway. Yet, he had to admit that They had rightfully shown repeatedly its necessity with this species and their deep rooted ignorance. Finally, with a great sigh, Brother John Plati turned to go back to the monastery he had made for himself in the abandoned mine.

Entering the domed alcove, he looked up at the huge stone cross hanging commandingly there and thought once more of the many who bowed to the symbol, yet the few who really believed and even less who practiced its ideal. Such shallow waters, these creatures, this species. So, despite his reluctance, he had understood from the onset that there had to be a renewal of Delusion in their near future.

Nonetheless, he could not help but wish They would not have to use the Power. How desperately he wished these beings would simply and sanely choose the Good as Aaron long ago told them; and, in truth, they came so close so often. But they would not, or could not choose it finally and it was foolish of him to stand here sighing at their symbols. Plati went into his study and began to call the Gathering.

The Assembly

Even the loud amplified screech of the microphone could not be heard over the louder hubbub of the shouting delegates at the Assembly for Sane Societies (ASS). The Chairman was shouting into the mike, "Please, please, ladies and gentlemen of this august assembly, please be quiet and remember the objectives of this distinguished organization." He banged the gavel but his efforts were interrupted by mad warring voices:

"Everything, and I do mean everything that Mr. Baddham says is a blot on my country and the good honest people there who make heroic attempts at peace."

Interrupted by Baddham: "Your peaceful county just blew up eighteen children at their play in my country. And further more, your MXX 2100 is built to hit all our bases in – – –"

Interrupted by: "Excuse me, sir and with all due respect, but I don't think with the stockpile of weaponry your country has aimed at us allows your accusations – – –"

Interrupted by: "That is a dirty filthy lie!"

Interrupted by: "You are the liar here and I..."

Interrupted by: "Everytime, constantly and without fail, when you come to these peace talks, your intent is only to manipulate."

Interrupted by: "If there was ever a nation with closets full of nuclear weapons that they use to manipulate, it is your nation! We know..."

Interrupted by: "Wrong, wrong, wrong, wrong. We are the only ones who honestly work for peace while your country continues, secretly it thinks, tests and prepares – – –"

Interrupted by: "Sir, I think you forget the purpose of ASS. We come together to bring some hope of..."

Interrupted by: "Ha, you sir, represent a nation that daily dares to insult this honorable ASS with your..."

Interrupted by: "How dare you suggest..."

Interrupted by the gavel and chairman shouting into the microphone, "Friends, Friends, truly we can have a workable ASS here if we all just try to cooperate and..."

Interrupted by: "I will not stand here and have my noble nation insulted by these calamitutidious calculations and draconary diversions that in fact make an ass out of ASS."

Interrupted by: "Oh, here the lady goes, resorting to language to mask the fact that..."

Interrupted by: "And I won't stand here listening to your sonorous mouthings and invented phrases verbally manufactured to create chaos to..."

One delegate of the peace conference took off his shoe and banged it on the rostrum, talked about burying nations as another retorted that they would see who buried who, and one by one, began stomping out of the peace conference.

The Gathering

He watched at They gathered in the quiet chapel. He had not seen some of them for seven centuries; some he had seen intermittenly through the ages, and some, like his beloved friend Arron Stocles, constantly. Regardless of the myths about their rarity, there were in fact, 1200 of Them, though only The Twelve were required for Gathering; and even The Seven could achieve the vote. These gathering now, though there would be serious conflicts and contentions, could and would, make the Decision if it was proven necessary for them to employ the Method.

He smiled as crotchety old Mathilde Sepsut came in glaring as usual. Hattie was always counting the number of women at Gathering and her purposive scowl spoke thoughts. Some teased her about it, reminding her that among Them, sexual politics had never been played. Besides which, she was free to transmute to any temporal or spatial condition she chose; but the constant mild rancor flavored her vinegary way.

Francis Goodman would agree with Hattie, however, as he did with everyone. The man was without ego and very little pride that could deface his placidity. Francis would defend Hattie, reminding Them that in light of contemporary thought, They should make more effort to see that six of Them at all gatherings be female.

Plati enjoyed the memory of each as they entered. Old Dan T. Alagrene stumbled in with his omnipresent morose look. He was living in England presently as, oddly, was Goodman. Many of Them had moved to the "blessed isle" since the Sixties, though Arron and Josh stayed, as they should, in America. There had been a bit of a controversy over Alagrene's odd connections with those tow-headed rock boys, some of Them fearing that the mysticism of the boys might lead to Their Discovery. Dan contended, and ultimately it did seem that the association was natural. Dan remained close to the boys until the murder, when he, as he often did, withdrew unto himself for some years. Like Prometheus, Dan's sympathies had been a concern through the ages; many felt that he often risked making unacceptable revelations to the creatures. There had even been some attempts to contain him, but to no avail. Dan remained the always singular, always at seeming mid-life, isolate and celestial, but unlike

Francis Goodman, grounded on the planet.

Josh Crates, though residing in Alexandria, Virginia, to keep an eye on things was always very careful around capitols. Fact was that the old slovenly crow spent considerable time at Virginia Beach ogling the young bodies of both sexes. From there, he was in close enough contact with Plati in the West Virginia mine-monastery that they could quickly contact and plan for anything. Josh's joviality made him a natural everywhere. From time to time in the bizarre Sixties the grand old man's leadership had come to the forefront among the young hippies, and even Josh had to be warned to use restraint. But once again, as in the previous era, there had been accusations of his corruption of the young and some officials wanted him removed from the city.

Leaning in close to hear what Josh was saying was Lizzie Angland. She had usually objected to meeting in the new country, claiming it was still too young, but the Others accused her of sour grapes dating back to the 1770s. Lizzie's long relationship with Mac Villion, on again-off again, made Italy her favorite country. Though also naturally opposed to both Constraint and Method, Lizzie had the knowledge and great respect for Necessity and would readily invoke it if a Decision was drawn. It was obvious that she wanted to conclude gathering quickly so she could be as far from Arron Stocles as possible. She had also had a brief fling with him when she was very young, but they became adversaries afterward.

Villion was of course in attendance and though there were objections because of his constant contentiousness, Villion would bring the necessary balance so essential for Decision. To oppose him, ever, was Jeff Thompson and Katrina Romano, for differing reasons. Iris Osisian would always be there to suggest compromise.

Plati turned and smiled just as Tao-Chuang entered. Their smiles met. Tao still lived in the Old Land, barely recognizable to his memory, so changed and yet, somehow, changeless. Brother Plati nodded a sign of peace to them all, "August Ones of the Light, I greet you."

"As we greet you, Select." All said in Unison.

The Red Oval Room

"I warn you." The vitrolic man shouted, his face becoming crimson, his veins bulging in his throat and temples.

"And I warn you." The other man shouted, his face reddening, his veins bulging in his throat and temples.

"That strip of land has belonged to our people for all time," the man blared viciously.

"God gave us that land before time," the other man blared viciously.

The strip of land being claimed was in fact an ancient strip of land with the misfortune of containing some natural resources.

The Gathering

"Sharers of the Light, you know of course, that it has become Necessary to Gather." Brother Plati was saying, "You know our reluctance to ever call you away from your various lives and studies. Besides, we know you are all saddened as are we to come to this consideration. Let us begin in Silence."

Silence among them had a heft, almost a weight as if of thunder but the moment it ended Arron Stocles began, "I must open this Gathering by saying emphatically that I don't think we ought even to bother with these inane stupid creatures this time."

It was the expected opening and got the expected response from Iris Osisian, "Arron, you know I am considerably older than you and don't grin because you're thinking, Iris is older than God's imagination." Arron smiled at the old crone's harangue, "I happen to be just old enough to be one of those who still can question your wisdom, because I saw it being born." Arron felt her inner mind which said, "I caused it being born."

"For example," Iris continued audibly, "I wonder if you even really understand Necessity at all." She slipped into the contemporary-vernacular, "Like, give us a break, Arron, as these beings used to say. You know Brother Plati would never have disturbed the comfort and peace of our Dispersal unless Gathering was unavoidable. And recall, there were times when we had to meet annually."

"I didn't mind the trip at all, Brother." Francis said, "These mountains are beautiful. What do they call them? Appalachian, I believe. I never heard that name until you moved here."

They never interrupted one another and Arron had waited impatiently for Francis to finish the unrelated nonsense; the man could use a course in categories, "But, Iris, we met annually because we were embryonic and thought was new. We and they, at least to some point, were to evolve intellectually. To Gather now is to move backward."

"We have to serve them, Arron," Lizzie said. "You often approach this as if it were a choice. As if it were not the unalienable duty of the superior to serve the interior." Thompson had grimaced at the word; he was propriatorial about the word, "unalienable", but continue listening, "Service to the servants; every master has taught that."

"I can't accept that when they threaten to bring us down to the levels. I think Gathering, even once in two hundred years is interruptive when we have so many concerns. Besides which, we all find this type Decision disruptive to our own natures. After all, all our work and private study is chiefly for their benefit also, so it's easy to argue that it's interruption is reprehensible. And of course, we will continue to go on aiding them though they prove themselves worthless time and time again."

"What a very Arronic thing to say." Francis spoke with a strength and firmness that had never ceased to startle them for eight centuries, "Whatever their flaw, they are not worthless."

Though he, too, was generally among his opponents, Plati felt compelled to defend his old pupil, "Arron, it's natural that we all tire of them from time to time. But I know you, too, feel committed to do what is best for them."

"Forgive me, and with all due respect, but I've long considered the idea of abandoning them altogether." Iris gasped audibly at Arron's admission and others evidenced near disbelief. "The time, talent and energy their ignorance saps from us no longer seems worth it."

Plati had feared this; that the chaos of division among the simpletons might eventuate in a replica of division Within. Some did not fear it. Some even doubted that there could be a real virtual separation to the Unity. But Plati believed that chaos was more powerful than that and it was that fear that had delayed his call to Gathering. Ever since the creatures had learned the first crude elementary processes of the nuclear arts, there had been Division in the μ υ σ τ η ζ.

Arron was not the only one who felt that they should be left alone to this own futile foolish ends.

"But they're so helpless," Francis offered.

"On the contrary. In any era, even the most ignorant of them, especially the most ignorant of them, master the forms of destruction. It's construction they're impotent with. And don't look like that, Francis. Gentleness won't work with them either. Many of their greatest evils are performed in its name."

Before Francis could protest the unfairness of the statement, Villion stood up, "I agree with Arron. Since 1945, after I observed their imbecility in Japan I thought we should Gather."

"I admit that I thought they might destroy themselves before our experiment in politics was even fully launched in history," Thompson said.

"But that was over fifty years ago. You have to admit they seem to want to contain that ability."

"Because they are afraid, Francis! Not because they care, or are insightful." Villion went on. "That's the only thing that works for them. You know that to be true. The point is, that more and more of them, not just nations, but small splinter groups..."

"They call them terrorists." Arron offered; he and Villion spoke as a unit.

"Precisely that. Oklahoma City is just the beginning. And these little morons have the information now..."

"Mac is correct. You can't call it knowledge if they possess it."

Francis, Alagrene and Iris all seemed to feel personal pain at what they knew was Villion's accuracy. "And in those hands, it is very possible. I think if they're so determined to self-destruct again, let them! This time they really know how. These cretins have been acting like this since before Crete----"

"Forgive me all, but I am compelled to interrupt. Villion, if you have to continue the tirade, at least stop this name-calling."

"Francis, I am genuinely sorry. I do apologize to you. But I find them to be as so many great giant fleas feeding off the bodies of our aspirations and inspirations. And there's no need to try to deflect the truth of what I say be telling me I sound like one of their Neitzsches or Hitlers because facts will remain facts no matter who calculates. Yes, they pick through our accomplishments without comprehension. All of the towers of the spiritual knowledges we give them remain, for them, either suspect, or superstitions or tools to try to make their God-concept kowtow to their demands. They sort through what we produce and use only what they want for entertainments or weaponry. Then, they ask for more of those. They pester us with inane pretensions, and as Arron says, they are just not worth it."

"Too much, Mac," Thompson spoke. "Like all your appraisals, though there's some truth, it's just too much. Your assessments are clever, but single-minded and I must add, aristocratic. Of course, they don't grasp absolutes, but they do aspire to them. I think they'll learn eventually."

"We've had that sort of crap from you for a couple of centuries, Jeff, while they all but wrecked civilization with it. All this century has left, of dignity, honor, integrity, values and that ilk, are the shards."

"They build, too. They strive toward us, don't you see that. We just have to wait for their understanding."

"I think you're having us on again, Jeff. Do you think these grunting belching snorting shouting blobs of bestiality..."

"That's too much, Mac," Plati breathed a sigh of relief that Arron had said that before he had to. He was losing count of the number of interruptions amoung them now as Villion added: "Call them what you will. Do any of us think these beings, totally satisfied in ball stadiums gorged with hot dogs and beer, long for essence."

"I do." Francis and Thompson spoke the credo together. Villion walked over the Thompson. Though equals, Villion had never been able to understand this man and his curious twist of mind, democracy? Let rabble rule? Result: rubble. Here was a philosophy that by its nature promoted the common, the minimum middle, the average, all bringing the "aristos" downward. "You'll forgive me, Jeff, but sometimes I find you as foolish as Francis."

"I do not allow that, Villion!" Plati's stern voice chilled the Gathering and brought an instant silence. All took offense with him and Villion quickly apologized. As he sat down, Lizzie whispered to him, "You sound like the creatures-in-assembly, Mac. Honestly, sometimes one would take you for a member of ASS."

"It's all right," Jeff said in his friendly manner, raising the sign for peace, "Let's not get tense. I understand Mac's reservations. I'm not blind to their faults. I just think we have to keep in mind that those faults are occasional and at other times, they love, care and think."

"Think." Arron made a cautious defense for Villion, "I often rethink the categorization of them as homosapien."

"That's not as funny as if should be." Lizzie, too, was feeling defensive. "How call them thinking when war and conflict seems to be a reasonable resolution for them. They find chaos acceptable and apparently judge insane society, sane."

"It seems to me they most definitely do not see war and conflict as reasonable solutions." Dan said.

"I'm not finished, Dan. Not since the Darkness have children been more at risk. And then, they use their domestic and relational horrors as television entertainments, as "movies of the week". Politically they are so abyssmal that they hardly even note the fact. Ethics are negotiable; corporations respond only to money or legal threats and everyone has a legal threat while the legal system dances with the lowest common possibility."

"Now, Lizzie, we've seen all this in history before."

"Never with such increasing acceptability, Iris, no."

"I refuse this for them. They don't accept it. Their voices are screaming."

"Francis, there are none so blind as they who won't see. They have among those screaming voices those who find nuclear annihilation thinkable."

"Few!" Francis resisted.

"It would only take a few." Mathilde finally spoke.

Thompson's face was growing more concerned as the conflict grew among Them: "They really can't help it. It's in their nature. Which is, finally, our own."

"Exactly, Jeff." Villion was up again, "That's the point. As enlightened as we are, as knowing, we have been ones to accept small wars, errors and foibles. I recall many occasions when Brother Plati has even had to call a Peace or an Apology among Us. But the difference is, we attend! They continue."

"I disagree."

"Disagree! Disagree! Francis, when after the two incredulous wars of this century and the half dozen others they treat as peccidilloes; after the holocausts, the mass murders, the list too long to list, you disagree? They appear to study history, but then they repeat it and repeat it as if they're illiterates. And now, they are potentially able to end history."

"Perhaps," Thompson muttered resignedly, "Perhaps."

"Perhaps? Jeff, it is self-evident."

"Now now now." Josh Crates was up on his feet with his hands folded over his rotund belly, "... let's see if it's all that bad. That's why we're here. To insure against it's becoming so." He looked at old Tao, "We are, after all, some of this and some of that, are we not?" Josh started to laugh which led to his cough, "Darned if I don't still get some congestion from that concoction they had me drink."

μ υ σ τ η ς

Josh achieved the desired levity, but Aaron was impatient. He respected Josh but sometimes found him foolish, too. If they had not rapidly retrieved Josh, those archaic diminities could have actually terminated him. And now, here was Josh, claiming they had validity.

"No. At their best, they're mechanics. Perhaps expert, but mechanics nonetheless. Science suggests a love of knowing, a search for meanings." Arron had quoted his favorite poet for the last few centuries, "Let them assume a value system if they have not one." They hold seminars on 'science without ethics', for heavens sake." Arron was revealing a seldom shown emotion, "I am appalled."

Plati, more than any knew the rarity of Arron's mood; nor was he surprised by Alagrene's near whisper, "Sometimes, Arron, I think you yourself would annihilate them."

"No." Arron himself found his response too quick.

Katrina Romano joined the foray, "I'm not ashamed to admit it. It is both thinkable, and understandable that we should think about it."

"You would think so," Iris told her, "But it is unthinkable." Iris' voice soft, sad, disappointed but warm, the oldest among them; she always attended Gatherings and her position seldom varied: "No matter what errors they make, they are children."

All but lost in thought, Plati added, "And yet, Mother, now they do have a most dangerous 'toy'."

"Why go on like this. We're here to consider Method. Let's do that."

"No, Villion, I don't agree to that." Arron said, "Method includes Distortion that reduces us as well as them. There is nothing in them worth us. Their eyes are just holes; they don't even suspect our existence. "Illuminati", ha! The term is only the lunatic definition of a few of their drugged drones and ufoers and that is as close as they get to virtual reality."

"Arron, I have never heard you talk like this."

"Plati, I am exhausted with the effort they take. Their pididdingly little minds never surmount their egos. They create, under the awesome name of philosophy, aridities like "existentialism" and dare claim from the majestic conclusions we give them about essences, that we are in error because they can't conceive the concept. Give them ethics; they make rules. Give them Olympics; they make sports and bets. Give them insights; they create situation comedies; Give them technologies; they create video games, and I could go on ad infintem."

"You always did." Francis' lips curled with a smile. "And why do they call us 'illuminati', because they recognize and long for and seek in fumbles, the good, the true, the beautiful and the light."

"At best," Villion meant to continue Villion's litany, "they're beasts of burden. No, Francis, the proffered ideals of love and humanity don't change them and now they could end all in their suicidal forays of self-hatred. They pollute all spaces. They eat plastics and chemicals and then wonder where the cancers come from. They declare nutritional war on their bodies, beat them to thin them after their gluttonies and push pills down for the self-control because they have no self-discipline at all. They hate themselves, pure and simple. And now they have the ultimate weapon to use against that enemy."

Though a little more sadly, Arron again agreed. "We have to admit it. All we gave, taught and hoped for them has all been either ignored or turned to entertainment. There are no values left, or few, Francis, I see you bristling, a few values may be left. But they love horror, even you won't argue that. Consider their "art", Halloweens I, II and III, and yes, I know that's not the whole of it, but my lord, Kreugers are heroes among them; chainsaw murders are funny. I saw three young women on television recently, apparently not yet raped or mugged or had family so killed, who said "a little sex and violence in film and television is healthy."

"Exactly, and the exceptions are too exceptional. They perpetrate this as fun and then look back and can't understand how an Auschwitz happened to their noble species. The best minds of them are howling, spending jism as the spew and sperm of poetry, or they're cartoonists. The best thought of the century came from the cartoons, yes, they "have met the enemies and they are us." Unlike himself, Villion was dismayed by the look on Francis' face, "Francis, I wish they were all you. I wish they were capable of understanding how precious they could be."

The thought brought another self-invoked silence on the twelve. In its interim, Plati assessed: That Katrina was upset with him for allowing the conflict to go so far; That Iris was upset because he did not make his position clear; That Tao was the only one with him in knowing that this Point-Counterpoint had to be.

Alagrene broke the silence, "Be fair. Your strength blinds you to their weaknesses, Arron. You don't see how hard they try."

"That has always been your error, Dan. You always excused them."

"No, I just did not let the fact that they were flawed blind me to the fact of their humanity. And I never hated them."

"You honor their flaws. And I never hated them. You can only hate an equal."

"Like us." Villion was smiling at Arron, "Though I've always felt you were hostile to me. Odd, in that I think myself your heir."

"You're wrong there. Except for Neitzsche, I'm the most misinterpreted one among us."

"Brother John," Iris spoke softly but firmly, "With respect, I feel the need to remind that we are here to reach Accord. That we are the ones who advocate the consideration of opposites, and you Arron, the king of the concept of the Middle, the compromise. How then do we stand here and allow the elements of discord this freedom of reign?"

Without words, Tao offered concordance with Iris and before others could concur, Arron and Villion both offered the Apology and the meeting resumed. Thompson, attempting levity said, "You two are just being rash." Arron took it as an affront but with the freshly invoked Union, let it go as Thompson continued, "I admit to much of Arron's assessment of them and that yes, sometimes they can be unthinking. I recall when the writers of chthonic made up myths and fairy tales to entertain them..."

"They make gods of them. I'm sorry to interrupt but I feel too strongly about it."

"So, made gods of lightening and thunder, Mac." Mathilde came to their defense, "They had fears and they responded as best they understood, I don't find that reprehensible. And recall, some of them deify earth and all this goes to show that they do recognize some principles of awe and Mother, even if some of the rituals are foolish."

"I'd give them that truth about the Mother if they hadn't gone on to rape her." Arron said, "That's the great mystery where I'm concerned. They have all but canonized their ability to destroy. They take the awesome Mother image and hacked it down to an endangered hag of abused land. On top of which, their gods now are all metallic, technique, and electronic; they don't accept anything but matter."

"I know, and understand how you feel about them, Mother." Lizzie consoled Mathilde, "And perhaps the primitives did have an awe of earth, and honor for seed and grain, but these new allegedly erudite sophisticates turn even the beauty of wilderness into steel and concrete."

"Must this go on?" Francis asked.

"It must if we are to make a Decision," Mac continued. "We find them vulgarians who leave nothing virgin. They laugh at the very idea of virginity. Their music roar; their talentless poets screech and scream the same line over and over again for want of lyrics and they plug such screech into their ears so that even by these they cannot hear the wonder of the endless waves. They slaughter small defenseless animals and call it "sport." From the most elevated scriptures, they conclude that they are crowned with "dominion" and use it as a privilege over their fellow creatures. They are violent! All they have retrained from the first breath, is violation!"

His eloquence compounded by the truth of what he said was so overwhelming that even Francis would not respond for a moment. Then Katrina Romana rose majestically, "They should never have been given even a modicum of information. I always said it. And these --- democrats"... she gave Thompson a contemptuous look, "... and this smaltz about the common rule have now achieved just that end."

Mathilde was musing on losses; the ibis and eagle, the matterhorn, endangered whales and eels; and she spoke reluctantly, "Perhaps you're right. Information is all they seem to have. They do not appear to have risen above the informational level."

The obvious statement gave rise to general hubbub. Plati grew concerned that Decision might come quickly, leaving the creatures totally to themselves for a time, this time. He listened as even Dan began the surrender, "Maybe we should have frozen them in the Eleventh Century, when it was suggested."

"Exactly. They were content enough then. Happy."

"No, Villion, they were not happy. Let's not drown in your simple semantics. You were always philosophically careless." Josh said.

"At least they had some respect then! For themselves. For us. For work and ideals."

"That's outrageous, Lizzie, we controlled them." Plati had avoided this as long as he could, but now felt under compulsion, "Every choice they made was made in fear. Superstition ruled them."

"Superstition then; drugs now. The results are always the same. I have concluded, after considerable inner deliberation..." None of them would deny the truth of that in Arron,"... and I repeat, they are not worth our time, even worth the time we spend to gather."

"Worthless. Then I suppose you might choose their semantics and 'waste' them?"

"We don't waste them, Jeff, they do. At least in what they called the Dark Age, ha, and I have to laugh when this benighted century calls another dark..."

"Just make your point, Mac."

"My point, Brother Plati, is that at least in those long ago eras of faith, even with their visions of sizzling frying pans, they did behave. But these current ignorant pomposities think they know. Their alleged scientists destroy faiths by the churchful and convince these maudling masses that they have explained Infinity, the unknowable. They have come to actually think that their frail failed finite minds can grasp the Source. Their insipid scholars call themselves agnostics, even atheists, as if they could conceptualize such concepts."

"Excuse me," Plati interrupted, "But I must call Point and Time on you. I hear such hostility that I think I must, in fact, question judgement."

Using all the control he could muster, Villion said no more. Plati called for justification of the Opposite and Arron forced himself to state the same: "We must admit that it was not only fear and superstition that made them behave. They do seem to suspect Harmony. And I think they may have --- a sense of love."

Mathilde said, "Remember that they accepted bodhisattvas and the cristos among them, though they do personify them. Still, at least they sought, even if archtypically and in some physical or concrete form, the Absolutes."

"Enough, We must reach Point, and quickly." Katrina huffled, "We all know they approach, have long done so, an acceptance of self-annihilation." She gave both Arron and Mac a stern look, "I believe we have belabored that point."

"I don't even accept that much. Recall that all their videos and games and fictions suggest to them that they will survive nuclear holocausts."

"And Dan, could they be more stupid than that for you? What – and I repeat – WHAT ever would survive, whatever type of mutant might remain would hardly be defined 'human'." Lizzie said.

"You forget their peace movements." Francis reminded them.

"A couple of soft voices, with guitars, whispering beside their holocausts." Iris admitted sadly, "We should never have stopped the Mysteries."

"Those were not absolute truths." Katrina said.

"And yet," Iris added, "they contained truths. Katrina, even you should know the value of that. They were truths that the beings could absorb. And, most importantly, the Mysteries kept them in awe."

"Fear."

"Fear stands twin to awe, and the two stand in good stead. They had reverence and with that lost, they lack the qualities that feed, nurture and sustain the human spirit."

"We didn't abandon them, Iris." Mac was ignited, "They so misunderstood even the kykeon of Mystery as to make it only a drug among them. In their assimulated ecstasies they didn't even seek true essence. When the first existential came along, put a little Sartre in their beer, and they bought it without even a dip in depth."

"I say they intend the Good." Francis' voice became strained as he saw the approach to Decision growing stronger, "Yes they fail, yes they're flawed, but they aspire!"

"You of all of us, know better. Give them christos and they crucify. The grand truth contained in cross becomes a sword with which to slaughter in what they call a 'holy land'. There, they all kill and conquer for their separate ideas of God."

"Don't you feel for them at all, Mac?" Josh asked, "Poor creatures of a day. They're so brief and that knowing can make them ignorant and self-indulgent. Remember, we were them. Regardless of the e-t stories and pyramid-building-cosmos-visitors, don't forget who we are."

"That's precisely what I don't forget." Mac's calm stern voice belied the fact that he was preparing to ask for Point, "I remember how we worked. How we studied and struggled to teach them. I remember how we've had to adopt even the unsavory when we learned that it was truth, yet they belly-ache, holding us behind."

"I tell you again that is the result of knowing they are so brief."

"Death, Josh, don't use their euphemisms and don't let their cheap muleishness creep in among us. The word is death, not brevity. And they lack self-discipline. Even when we've shown them the harm in what they eat and drink, they do toward death like automatons. Smoke, ha! They are death-mechanics and absolute fucking idiots..."

A hard physical silence fell on the Gathering at the profanity as Mac whispered, "I'm sorry."

"We've met the enemy. And they are us." Arron quoted.

Lizzie offered what she thought was a feeble defense, "Mac's tastelessness proves the axiom. Even we who drew the blueprints for Unity can be divided the moment we begin to consider them. They so mix the sacred with profane that we get caught in the web. Reason has to be perverted when you keep listening to ideas like 'Bombs for peace'. Remember their plans for the neutron bomb. They could conceptualize a weapon that would end every life form, every insect and leaf while leaving their steel and concrete standing, and you think fuck is a profanity."

"But they walked away from it." Francis was desperate now, "Think how so many resisted the Asian War and though there was little media coverage, there were many voices shouting against the Gulf War. They are trying to ease the anguish in Bosnia and Rwanda..."

But the mention of the neutron bomb had effected Thompson, "I hate admitting it. They haven't done what we thought they would."

It was followed by a string of comments:

"They are always at war, or looking for one."

"They don't seem to care."

"Respect is a comedian's need."

"They are getting better and better at getting worse and worse."

"They may be, finally, uneducatable."

"I see little real improvement since Crete."

"And yet." All stood up, for this the ever-silent voice of Tao, "I seem to love them."

The Great Room

The meeting was more quiet than usual.

Now that those words had actually been articulated; emotions ran high and mixed; some felt terror, some excitement.

"We can't destroy them."

"We can."

"Then, do we do it?"

"I don't know."

"I have no reservations whatsoever."

"To hell with them. We've agreed they won't listen."

"Let's do it then."

"It'll be like last time. We didn't win then."

"We didn't lose."

"We came close."

"Enough from this lily-livered liberals, let's blow them up!"

The Gathering

The meeting was more quiet than usual; from Powers, they

had just realized the decision made in The Great Room. Now that their words had been articulated; emotions ran high and mixed; some felt terror; some excitement.

"Do we destroy them?"

"That was never a consideration."

"Then, do we do it?"

"I don't know. I have some reservations."

"I have none."

"Let's begin."

EPOPTAI

They said their final prayers and blessed Light.

Brother Plati called for final statements and he began: "I don't like controlling by fear."

Josh, "I dislike using illusion on them."

Arron, "It's what works with them."

Mathilde made the difference, "As Tao, I too see the Necessity."

Thompson unhappily spoke the motto and all twelve responded. Decision was made and Method, as usual, was left for Arron.

Method

Pam Burchett was about to turn off the roast in her microwave when the great light came and almost blinded her. So great was the brightness that it seemed to physically throw her against the wall.

Howard Milton had just been admitted to Clark General Hospital in Ona, West Virginia, and was turning off his television when the light engulfed his room with its brilliance.

Little Olga Kromanovski was in the middle of her childish fight with Nena Baranaski and was about to pull her hair again when the whole outdoors around her lit up and her house seemed bathed in celectial light.

In Piltdown, England, Phil Jones was mowing his lawn; in Narobi, Ote Kone was telling her neighbor some gossip; in Canton, China, Lin Tse-Ching, eighty-six and blind from birth began to weep as the light entered his eyes; Ingrid Holbert dropped her groceries; Abdul Kimir turned off the engine on the tank and in El Salvador, Sister Maria saw it and was not surprised, but still knelt and screamed with joy.

The Great Room

As the light broke into the room:
"Oh, my God, look, look outside!"
"It's entering the room."
"What can it be? What's causing it?"
"Maybe it's one of their tricks."
"Or a gas explosion."
"Not with this much light."
"Could it be some sort of light refraction?"
"What if the myths we tell are truth?"
"God? After all?"
"Look, the lights growing."
"I've never seen anything like it."
"We don't have anything that can destroy it."
As the light completely engulfed the room, several of them fell to their knees; some crossed themselves and most began to mutter unfamiliar prayers:
"Oh God, what can we do?"
"It's nothing."
"It's something."
"Do you think they did it?"
"They don't have this capability. Nor do we."
"We had better get them on the phone. Let's see if they see it."
"Exactly. We are going to need their help."
"They may need us."

Diaspora

The light was dimming to twilight as the four stood looking at the sea.
"I've always loved the sea."
"Now maybe the beings will see it again. Hear it."

"I know they will. They are already becoming so prayerful. There's even some silence among them."

"True. And as usual, Arron, your Method worked. They're uniting."

"Yes." Arron sounded sad, "But you know, I hate the illusion, too."

"John, you were the first to perceive how dimly they saw."

"And yet, left to me, I don't know if I would ever use the Method."

"Regardless that on their own, they won't even turn away from the darkness of the cave."

"But this light, Arron, it just frightens them."

Knowing how uncomfortable Arron was, Josh came to his defense, "At least, fear brings them together. If love and common cause, and natural mutuality does not fuse them, then fear. Mac's no fool, you know. We all know love is best, but fear always works." Josh shoved his hands in his pockets and studied the sea.

"How long do you think you'll have to continue Illusion, Arron?"

"I'm not sure we should ever lift it again."

"But it's control, it reduces them. They have no will."

"Yes. But at least they continue, John. At least there's some potential, some hope."

Plati was about to object again, but realized that the fear and the light brought them awe, and with it, revival of the sense of majesty and mystery. They had lost that. In their ego-centricity they had lost the actuality of vastness, with their small foot on the moon, some thought they had conquered those antique and eternal mysteries; thought they would defeat time and space.

> Tao continued in silence as the four looked at the sea, listening. Then, the four dispersed; each going in different directions.

And the light shines in the darkness
but the darkness cannot overcome the light

for
thought some love the darkness,
some come to witness
to testify to the light.

The Eligible

I

Ellie Ransom woke up at precisely 6 a.m.

As always, she thought. But then again, I am more or less clockwork.

Ellie turned toward the window where the summer sun leaked through the crack at the bottom of the window shade; a perfect morning. Ellie's vibrant body pulsed with vigorous life, forging an irresistible desire to leap up Belcher Mountain and begin dawn. Her warm blood surged like the wonderful clear crimson brook of life it was; she felt marvelously fit as she flung her limber legs over the side of the bed. Ellie stretched her honed arms, rippling the perfectly toned muscles as she reached toward the ceiling. And she felt miserable. Today was Ellie Ransom's birthday. It was the year 2180 C.E. and she was 196 years old.

"I am 196," she repeated aloud as her husband entered the room. Robert was already dressed in his maroon body-suit and for a moment Ellie had to admire that incredible two hundred-year-old body. But admiration quickly turned into something else. But what else? Ellie baffled herself because she could not define the "something else". But it was real, and increasingly it was her experience, a vague, vague need.

Ellie lifted her head slightly as Robert bent to kiss her cheek, "Happy birthday, my old wonderful-birthday-sweetie". He always spoke with laughter in his throat. After the cheery greeting, Robert bolted from the room and was off and running up Wolf Pen Mountain as he did each morning by 6:15 a.m. Their lives were as constant as each dawn and both of them would run ten miles before 8 a.m. Of course, such exercise was unnecessary as they were technically, digitally monitored so that their perfect bodies would be instantly corrected should the least inadequacy occur. That eventuality was inconceivable.

Ellie walked to the window just in time to see her seventh husband begin his herculean hurdles up the West Virginia hills in MCDW County. She did smile as Robert burst through the brambles like a buck. Once he was out of sight, Ellie turned and went to look at the calendar. It was a print of M.C. Escher. Her son had given it to them for the new year. This month's picture was "Ascending and Descending"; graphic depictions of stones and steps with forms and figures whose legs were poised in such illusory fashion that the viewer could not discern if they were going up or coming down the steps.

Apt.

Lifting the pages of the calender, Ellie stopped at "Drawing Hands". Painted in 1948; 152 years ago, Ellie could not quite believe in such times. Little knowledge of such eras were allowed, thus making the bizarre work all the more difficult to assimilate. Often, she had wondered at them allowing such paintings as this to continue to be reproduced. Looking at it you could not help but wonder what was in such a man's mind. Some had said that such poets, or artists as they were called did this "attempted creativity" because they sought immortality.

Such a thought was beyond Ellie's thinking as was the very fact that she was allowed to have such thoughts at all. She could not believe that they did not know what she was thinking. She stared at the left hand that appeared to be drawing the right hand that appeared to draw the left hand; circles and circles and circles. Odd concept that, circles.

The calendar pages fell back through Ellie's hand to "Ascending and Descending". Today was July Fourth, Independence Day of the Old Way. If one accepted this concept of time, it was 2180 A.D., the dating that maintained the meaningless Annos Domini. In keeping some of the Old Ways, the Order sometimes evidenced a bow to a status quo that did not always reflect their rationale. Of course, they carefully selected what was maintained, but Ellie more and more found some of it confusing.

Odd, she thought. A stab of fear as fiery as a firebrand pierced through her; how could she even be thinking such thoughts. She could not recall ever even thinking about a meaning of the A.D. designation, much less the notion "Annos Domini". What was happening to her mind?

Born in 1984 --- another bolt of fear as Ellie wondered what was happening. 1984? She never thought backwards. It was Prohibited. But now it had begun and one thought was leading to another. In spite of herself, she remembered that her parents had had an Escher calendar one year. But perhaps the memory was all right; because the FDO did allow some back-thought if related to the birth-times. FDO always commemorated the birth-times. Ah, that was what was happening this morning; they were somehow allowing some recall. She could almost remember bits and pieces of the 1990s; societies and governments world-wide were crumbling; breaking, falling through their foundations like the sound of crystal tinkling through the crevices of centuries. Morals had ended; standards and values were leveled to the common denominator; politicians were "for hire"; schools had lost authority and taken knowledge down to the lower rungs of accessible information; churches were loud, leaning toward entertainment; drugs lobomotized to the best of their chemical proficiencies those endangered with thoughts or feelings, and the social, political and religious institutions had surrendered to the Order without so much as a prayer or protest.

Ellie could remember back to when it had started because, for some reason, FDO had allowed her the memory. She recalled the average life span then as beginning to approach one hundred; laughable now, it was considered an achievement at the time. There was even some early morning talk show person who showed photos and made a great to-do about those who reached that cherished century mark.

She could even remember, as a child, actually wondering if she might live to see the year 2100; and if so, if she might live a year or two more into that century. And now here she was, in 2180, and more fit than she had been as a teen in the 1990s. IDZ!

Oh my god, IDZ! Ellie knew instantly that she was in a grave zone and tried quickly to change her mental state. The FDO classified IDZ as high-risk; how could she have allowed herself to think, feel in this area? Ellie could not answer her own question. Of the zenith state, Ellie shuddered with realization; she was virtually considering eligibility.

II

Eligibility.

No. What was happenning to her. Ellie would never want to be eligible. And to think such a thing on one of her Special Days was unthinkable. She needed to think positively; on your special days you could make any request you could conceive and FDO would grant it. You could not think of something FDO could not give. Anything except---.

That. And yet the thought was in her. And yes, she realized, that she was going to actually ask that today. She had decided before she fully realized that she had done so; she wanted to be eligible and if they did not judge her so she would---.

Ha, ha, ha, Ellie began to laugh uncontrollably at the thought, ha ha ha, if they didn't allow it she might kill herself. Her laughter subsided, became vague and Ellie began to exercise mind-set. Creating a proper mental landscape, Ellie stood still, firmed before doing complete PC. Ellie had mastered Psyche-Composition before it had been fully classified and had seldom failed at it. She centered in less than ten seconds while looking at the motto of the Federal Decision Office:

EVERYTHING IN EXCESS

In fact, Ellie Ransom was one of the few people left in the United States of Cosmoterra who retained MR of the original Greek axiom that had now been inverted by the Socio-Perfects for the "joyofall". And Joyofall was the anthem of the US of C. At fourteen, when most were choosing to accept the initial Partial Cerebral Lobotomy – towards total happiness; Ellie had been one of the rare exceptions who declined, postponing her PCL until her eighteenth year.

As there were still so many individual decisions being made before the millenium, the FDO seemed hardly concerned about the few exceptions that did not choose the usual early narcotic alleviation of certain historical and allegedly archtypical memories thought to be uncomfortable.

In the entire state of WVGian and singly in MCDW County, Ellie had chosen the limited Memory Retention. She had been advised that even partial retention would be painful; that she would thus have some information left about the entire history of racism, holocausts, wars, etc, and that these could remain in her memory, causing her sadness for years. Ellie never understood why she had made the choice of limited retention, but it seemed right at fourteen. Nonetheless, she had done so and her qualifications had been such that she was later allowed to teach the modified history course for some ninety years after she underwent the propter PCL procedure.

After ninety years of teaching Acceptable History, including two courses in Advanced Acceptable History, Ellie was encouraged by FDO to accept the Stop Rest Rejoice and Celebrate matriculation. With the advent of her SRRC, Ellie was given special honor status and an all but unprecedented Specific Positive Retention category. The latter was rare and distinguished, given when one's ninety years of performance included no errors, and their Psyche-Composition was considered so perfected that they were ordained among the Elite. Elites were usually chosen from only FDO and very seldom among the Generality. Being an Elite would make the request for Eligibility even worse.

Subsequently, due to the privileged permission granted Ellie, her initial Partial Lobotomy only removed the "negatives" of the socio-historical Information-fount. Ellie had been allowed to keep the positive information of the past: I.E., the humanities, benign philosophies and the arts (purged), sports, (purged, though not so extensively as the arts) etc. Thus, Ellie knew all the details of the ping-pong match held by non-aggressive Orientals in 1920, but she had never heard of Auschwitz.

Of course, friends and family felt that Ellie's degree of MR was altogether useless baggage; why carry around in anyone's mind any negative when there were so many Good Thoughts to be had. And her decision to accept Partial Retention after SRRC had been beyond comprehension at FDO. The latter had been, in fact, the prime reason for at least three of her separations and were a matter of constant comment from Robert. Ellie herself sometimes wondered why she could not just go with the joy, love, goodness and beauty programmed for her by the Socio-Perfects. EVERYONE in the US of C was happy, as her FDO guide constantly told her.

Possibly, Ellie's maladjustments did come from the limited MR she retained. Probably the very reason she realized that some retention was "allowed" rather than free choice, was due to that very retention that most did not have. And yet, if her MR was only the Specific Positive category, how was it she could recall even such a thing as the original Greek axiom. How could she remember such a phrase as "Nothing in excess", unless something was wrong with her apparatus. But that was beyond belief. How distorted was she becoming? And yet, what if her PC were flawed. What would that bring?

II

"Ah Ellie, how good to see you."

Ellie was startled as the beautiful young woman ran toward her with her hand extended in warm welcome; her thoughts had been so concentrated that she had walked to the FDO without realizing it. The young woman clutched her hands and pulled Ellie into her arms, hugging her in rich friendship, "How wonderful it always is to see you, dear Ellie."

Released from the flooding arms, Ellie stood back from the jovial face of Joy Fuller, the local FDO chairperson, especially devoted to Ellie Ransom's enjoyment and fulfillment. For the past eighty years, Joy had been delegated to care for Ellie's special days. Looking at her now, Ellie was again startled as she recalled a line from somewhere, someone unknown, a line that could not be, yet was, in her mind: To prepare the face to meet the faces that we meet.

What an incredible idea; as if someone would prepare the face before hand for meetings with other; Ellie smiled back gleefully at Joy -- her friend, Joy, her best friend, in fact. Then, Ellie had a flicker of mind in which she would see Joy without this degree of glee. Impossible. The flicker of vision was uncomfortable, whatever it's occasion; Ellie did not want it today. Could not have it today. She must not do anything that might prevent Joy's approval of her eligibility.

Ellie had to become eligible today!

And then, like a serpent's tongue flicking out at its victim, Ellie had another fleeting reflection: I have measured out my life in coffee spoons.

Now she knew she was malfunctioning. What a thought! Ellie worked to rapidly erase the thought in her mind before Joy could read it on her computer. Such a thought would receive an immediate classification of Extreme Abberition. An EA on her printout today would make serious consequences for Ellie.

Besides which, Ellie could not make heads or tails of the thought: I have measured out my life with coffee spoons, indeed!

Nonetheless, how would she be able to obtain eligibility, and for that matter, why did she now seek it so strangely. Why was eligibility not given as a consequence of the obvious error growing in her, that would have a certain logic. Ellie closed her thoughts as quickly and proficiently as she was able and composed herself, laughingly, "And Ms. Fuller, it's always wonderful to see you."

"Joy Joy Joy now!" the woman laughed, "There are no formalities among we who love and laugh and know happiness. And I keep reminding you to call me, just plain Joy. Really, Ellie, no one can understand where you get these ideas. 'Ms. Fuller' in deed." So slight was the edge in her voice that Ellie could barely discern it, "Do you know where you get those ideas?"

"No." Ellie was surprised to realize it, "No, they just sort of come out like that when I speak to an official."

Oh no, a renewed, barely suppressed frown crossed Joy's face at the word, "official"; the expression all but imperceptible to anyone other that Ellie whose apology was a plea, "I'm sorry. Really. Perhaps that was what used to be ---."

Ellie stopped in mid-sentence; "used to", another unacceptable phrase; she was adding error to error. Ellie could not remember having ever made so many mental slips; using a past tense such as that was always a giveaway to a faulty PC. If she were not more guarded, FDO might decide she had too much memory. Ellie might be classified "borderline negative" even before she could mention eligibility. And for "borderline negatives", there was only one solution: correction.

"Oh, I hope every little thing is just A-ok-all-right." Joy laughed whenever she spoke but her eyes glanced over at the scanner where Ellie's emotions were being monitored. Ellie could not tell if she was printing them out or not as she continued, "Everything should be wonderful for you. This is, after all, your High Special Day, so of course you can have any thought you want. I find nothing wrong with your thoughts. I used that phrase 'used to' once myself. There are certainly worse offenses than that. Ha ha, I bet you didn't know I taught Acceptable History myself for a while."

"No, I didn't know that."

"Oh yes, you and I are so very much alike. This is a wonderful moment and I just love you, Ellie."

"Thank you, and I love you, Joy. You are wonderful and I hope you have a good day, too. I'm so glad you're my Joy-guide for Special Days."

Looking out of the office window, Ellie saw many others gathering. Many. That was one of two numbers Ellie knew, many and few; FDO did not allow any more specific numbers than those two. They did, however, give other numbers from time to time, as they did other memories, though these were temporary and one was not allowed to keep them. For example, as her Most Special Day was approaching, they programmed her temporarily to conceptualize the number two; that there would be one day, and that there would be the next day and that together they would be this number two. They had given her her calendar so that she could actually see these numbers beneath the drawing: a 1 and then a 2.

And more excitedly, along with the two temporary numbers, they had given her the memory that a son from her own body had given her that calendar. Also, because of her status, she had been such partial memories as those icons: 1984 and 2180. But except for occasional flashes, soon forgotten, those icons had no meaning. It was needless to think about them anyway because they would soon be erased.

But, many and few, were always retained, so Ellie could conclude there were many outside. These would all be on Special or Most Special Days, and had come to the FDO to have them Meet Need for Special Days. For a moment, Ellie wondered if any besides herself would ask for eligibility. Joy had always made it sound as if one could search the Cosmoterra over, far beyond these Wvmountains and never find one person requesting eligibility. The red neon,
EVERYTHING IN EXCESS
behind Joy's desk gave the room a festive feeling and Joy said gleefully, "Now suppose you just tell me what desires you have that FDO can meet today."

Meet desire; not Meet Need; there was another mental infraction and Ellie knew she should not have recognized it as such. But Ellie knew the code: Meet Need; Meet Need; All Needs are met in cosmoterra. Ellie centered and said, "This is the Fourth of July, Joy."

Joy seemed actually not to note that she said Fourth of July, a prohibited number, instead of the acceptable Independence Day. She spoke as if everything was as usual, "It is that, and aren't we all just bubbly happy about it. Oh, it's going to be a great day. You cannot in your wildest imagination imagine what we have in store to insure your perfect happiness."

That was a test: "I have no imagination."

"What?" Joy was unable this time to hide the clenched-mouthed expression as her eyes scanned Ellie's emotions monitor. However, in a seeming instant she had reconsidered her strategy, dismissed it and said more gently: "As I was saying, we have a truly stupendous Extravaganza of Entertainments prepared for you by the Fun and Games Department. There'll be all your favorite music, feasts and fireworks, your own personal parade and parties..."

Listening to the alliterative litany, Ellie assumed Joy was reading from the word processor on her wristwatch; she decided to do a rapid, all but unknown verbal attack, "Joy, I know there is a committee on Content and Agape. I also know that, according to Cosomoterra Committee set up to review the mountain states and that that committee has recommended the day of one's birth be classified as a Special Personal Day, making it mandatory that my request be heard."

"Ha ha ha ha, why of course." Joy laughed a deep malignant roar of a laugh, "You know that we who are the whole cosmos and reside in the organization of FDO, always listen to a One."

"Exactly. And I am a One. I hope I don't sound defensive."

"Defensive is a negative."

"And I don't want to sound negative."

"I know you don't, dear dear, Ellie, You're so very precious to US. You do know how all of US at FDO love you, don't you?"

"I do. And I love all of you." Ellie smiled back cautiously. "But, Joy it is my birthday. I feel you know why I'm here."

Feel? Another slip and though Joy tried to laugh, she could only force a smile, "Now don't tell me all your presents didn't arrive from the Desire and Demand Department."

"DDD is always on time. I have everything."

"And all of your audios and visuals, all the virtual reality modalities, all your holographic equipment is intact, isn't it?"

"There has never been a malfunction in any equipment that I, or anyone I know owns, Joy."

Joy openly punched the keyboard a moment, talking as she did so, "All of the last year's movies are at your home, all the new shows from Broadway, London and Paris and of course you can fly to those locales if you prefer. There are flights out of Wvstate every seven minutes. Oh ho ho, look at this." Joy indicated the screen, "I see we have six simulated holographic hockey clubs scheduled for your lawn on Robert's Special Day. Now, that reminds me, I do have to contact Elysian Climate to make sure your lawn in properly iced for the occasion." Joy paused a moment and looked at Ellie, "I do hope the icing on the lawn won't be a problem for you. We could have a new lawn set out just beyond your east desk, fully grassed this afternoon---."

"The icing on the lawn is not a problem, Joy."

"I'm glad to hear it. We want to keep Robert happy and with a mind-set that will keep him just the way you like him."

"I like Robert well enough."

"I myself, personally, ordered the Supreme Dusk Disk over your region with the accompanying Key West Sunset Component, just in case there is some unforeseen weather error on either of your days."

"You know, Joy, I've never experienced unforeseen weather."

With barely muted irritation, Joy went on, "If you have another preference, we could arrange it. I once had the strangest request, you won't believe. Some man wanted rain, can you imagine? But we gave it to him. And if you happen to like a snowy scene, we can contact the Muscovian section and have the real snow brought in. But what about a New England autumn, they've been very popular lately. Or a Parisian spring. Of course we do sometimes experience some momentary delay with our space climate channel but..."

"There's no need to go on listing, really it's not about the gifts or games."

"Food. What about some new menus. I think you like Oriental. We flew in Chefs Ling and Nakado. As a matter of fact, they may be at your home even as we speak."

"The food is perfect. The entertainment is perfect. I feel perfect. Robert feels perfect. The new menus actually arrived last night and they were perfect. The latest cyberbeing you sent to serve us is perfect. She actually reads what we want before we get a chance to speak our minds, so that we have our desire almost before the desire. The foods are ambrosia, the wines are nectar but..."

Whether guise or reality, Joy accepted the praise, yet interrupted, "Well, that's just wonderful. I was afraid something was amiss when we do so want you to enjoy your Most Special Day without any limitation. We at FDO know that with only 250 Special Days a year, there could be special desires between them. We try to meet them if we suspect it is so."

"Believe me, Joy, we have literally everything we can think of. As a matter of fact, we get some special gifts we never would have thought of."

Joy appeared deeply touched, "That's a beautiful way to put it, Ellie. You have a winning way with words. Maybe you should process some poetry. Do you think you might enjoy being a poet for a while, you know we can arrange for inspiration. We could start your poetry-processing procedure this very moment, if you like."

"No." For some indecipherable reason, Ellie was appalled but she covered quickly, "Thank you."

Joy laughed some more but Ellie suspected the grimace inside because the agent got up and took Ellie by the elbow. Gently, as if she did not want Ellie to even realize she was being prodded toward the private sound-proof room. Ellie blurted while she believed some others were still watching them, "I came to ask about eligibility."

III

Ellie knew she had said the word loud enough to cause some of the people outside the building to look up at Joy's window. Parts of most interviews were on loud speakers, to "increase the union in Union"; for "he or she who separates is lost." As she was in mid-word, Joy had thrust Ellie into the sound-proof room and slammed the door closed. Yet, if she mentioned to Joy that she had thrust her into the room, Joy would have laughed and told Ellie that she seemed to have an imagination after all.

But Ellie knew she did not, could not, imagine.

Ellie watched in silence as Joy went to the bar and activiated the Mechanmixerman, who instantly fixed Ellie's favorite drink as quickly as it could be computed. Joy handed her the drink herself, "Mai Tai. With the special south sea island fruit you like flown in the past half hour."

Joy smiled and sipped her own drink; then said with concern: "You are receiving your own daily south sea island fruits?"

"I am."

"Good." Joy nodded, which activated the Mechanmixerman which brought over a tray of cheeses, pates, party breads, etc. "Now, if you'll just taste and select what you like, we'll send the cases over for you." Joy smiled as in conquest, "And I just remembered your charities. You can also select from the approved poor list and we will ship truckloads of goods and money to them from you. I must tell you though, I still have reservations about allowing the select-poor. Still, FDO finds philanthropy to be so pleasant that we do maintain the poor-pretense for you."

"I'm not even sure I'm charitable, Joy."

Joy was angry. All the guises were operative in her person, but Ellie knew she knew she was angry as she spoke in the controlling tone, "You are listed as charitable, Ellie. Now if I'm not mistaken, there was a special avocado dip created for you this morning. You can taste it now and if it meets with your approval we'll send the whole load to you and your charity. You can patent the recipe if you like."

"Thank you, but I can't possibly taste and select just now. I had the complete breakfast that the Food for Fun Department sent for my Day."

"No, you did not eat this morning, Ellie. I know you didn't. You did not even need to use the calorie-eliminator."

Real danger, "But I do appreciate your thoughtfulness."

"We try, Ellie, we do try so hard. You know if you have any concern at all about the calorie-eliminator, all you need do is use the special blend of teas we sent. They're processed to eliminate both calories and bad cholesterol so you don't even need to use the eliminator."

One hundred and twelve; Ellie eliminated the incredible number from her mind as quickly as she thought it, "I know. And to my knowledge, my weight has never ever changed and that is wonderful." But regardless of the risk, before Joy could divert the conversation again, Ellie said, "About eligibility."

With no perceptible emotion, tone or inflection, Joy sighed, "Oh, Ellie."

"I am sorry."

"Sorry." Joy said. The tone itself was chilling; she should

have been furious but instead began to giggle laughter as she punched the button and lowered a screen. Instantly, Ellie's life appeared on it; her history, family, warts, blemishes, studies, husbands, children, playground falls in a town called KIMBALWV, record of menses before her decision to control, etc. For the moment, neither woman spoke as a voice summarized Ellie. Afterwards, Joy turned to her happily: "Well, Ellie, I don't see even a hint of malfunction."

Ellie sighed, about to break down as she realized the odd bits of thoughts in her mind: I grow old, I grow old, I shall wear the bottom of my trousers rolled, do I dare to eat a peach, do I dare disturb the universe; oh please, what is happening to my mind, losing it, in a moment there is time, what nonsense, my life closed twice before it's close...

"No. Absolutely no apparent malfunction of parts at all."

"No apparent malfunction."

"None. So you must see how astonishing it is to hear you talk like this."

...grow old along with me, the best is yet to be, the winged chariot does not draw near, not with a bang but a whimper...

"I mean, Ellie, I am amazed. If I had some idea what could be troubling you, or what part of you is out of focus, I'd act on it immediately, but you are simply marvelous. Perfect. So what else could you want that..."

...since childhood's hour I have not been as others were, my passions I could not bring from the common spring and all I loved I love alone...

The deepest silence Ellie had ever known physically engulfed Ellie as Joy read her last thought on the screen. She could tell by her eyes that the words were as meaningless to Joy as they were to herself.

Meaningless, and yet---I feel them.

The brittle dry laugh of Joy's was intentionally evoked to suggest to Ellie how hard it was for her to believe that Ellie was asking again in spite of the recent trauma; still Joy smiled: "FDO is always ready to hear requests."

"I don't like to be a bother."

"What an unusual thought. No one in all Cosmoterra is ever a bother."

"I mean, I haven't even let myself think about it since last birthday. I did repress, as you enforced."

"As I suggested. And you haven't thought about it since last birthday because you can only ask for eligibility on birthdays, but no matter." Joy bit out a laugh, "And let me be completely honest. I personally don't feel Ones ought to be able to raise the question of eligibility, Special Day or not." Joy continued to smile her friendly smile, "I happen to be among those at FDO who think complete control, even the thought of eligibility ought to be eliminated from Ones."

"I'm sorry. I don't think I understand any more why you resist."

"As I have never understood at all, your request."

"Why is it a problem?"

"Where do you find these questions?"

"You have to answer me today, why is it a problem?"

"Because it is a risk."

"How? Why? You always say I'm the only one who ever requests eligibility, so how can it be a risk?'

"It just is." Joy laughed merrily. "And do be precise, dear. I did not say no one requested. I said, few did."

"Then some do request?"

"Few."

"Are any allowed?"

"Ellie, you know good and well only Malfuncts are chosen."

"How many last year?"

"Where do you get ideas like that?"

"'Many' is allowed and 'few'."

"But the way you use them is not allowed, Ellie! You are making an evaluation! You are suggesting numbers!"

"Joy, it's my Most Special Day."

"You are never allowed such questions."

"In fact, less than fifty in the whole Cosmoterra were allowed eligibility last year."

Joy could not suppress her surprise, "Who gave you number?"

"Someone made an error in one of the computers sent to me. In a rather elementary way, I entered the term --- Depression."

"Ha, you're bluffing. There's no such term."

Ellie realized that Joy really did not know the term, "I have certain recollections."

"Inadequate PCL!!" Joy shouted angrily; and smiling, slammed the desk, "I've told them it would come to this. Those of you allowed to retain, even the past positive memories, you will always end up with these unnatural desires from eligibility."

"Why no, Joy? Can fifty-one people matter? Just one more. You have my clone prepared. I know it. I'd be right back and this other me would probably never make the request."

Joy finally lost complete control; the smile was defeated, "You are not eligible to die, Ellie. Do you hear me! You're not going to be allowed. There's no reason for it."

All Ellie's hopes began to fade; measured out in coffee spoons, by mermaids tenanted, whatever, confusion; Joy's decison would be final with FDO and still Ellie said, "Please."

"I can't. I can't even understand your asking." For a fleeting second, Ellie felt that Joy wanted to understand as she added, "I mean, you almost make me sad. If there is such a thing."

"There is such a thing and I know it, Joy and it's not so awful."

"You do not know the sad! You can't! You're only a hundred and ninety-six years old. They were conquering pain and sadness while you were an infant. It was gone by the time you were thirty. They eliminated it from your memory before 2020..." Joy stopped; she had told more than any Joyful adept had ever told before.

Ellie confessed: "I don't know them, Joy, but I know their definitions. To be sad is to be "affected with an expression of grief and unhappiness, downcast, causing or associated with grief or unhappiness, depressing, deplorable, regretted. It is, in fact, to experience a series of negatives..."

The rage that now consumed Joy broke dams in Ellie's mind: jug jug jug, Ellie thought as Joy picked up the definitions, quoting them like a robot speaking from a memorized script: "To be pain is as punishment, usually localized physical suffering associated with bodily disorder, as in a disease or injury; a basic bodily sensation induced by noxious stimulus, received by nerve endings, characterized by physical discomfort. What a horrible definition, Ellie, can you want that?"

"No, of course not. Listen, this, to be death, is not like that."

"Listen Ellie, to be death is 'permanent cessation of all vital functions, the end of life, lacking power to move, tell, or respond; incapable of being stirred emotionally or intellectually, grown cold, extinguished, inanimate, inert to mention only a part of the qualities of to-be death. What earthly cause would one have to seek such a state?"

"I don't know the answer."

"You don't know. You actually come here asking for to-be-death, this annihilation, this cessation of sensation and you don't know why?" Ellie had no response as Joy hammered thoughts, "Do you know how hard the Socio-Perfects work and study to bring us to the state we now are in?"

"Yes. I know better than you. I lived through Development, you were born heiress to it. I have begun to remember the talk of the first artificial heart, a man named Barney Clark, just before I was born. It was a faulty first step but there were those even then who thought it would result in the ability to replace all the parts."

Startled, Joy said, "Why, you must remember – cancer – AIDS – e boli."

...slings and arrows of outrageous fortunes; all flesh is heir to; Shakespeare and Hitler, oh what is happening, I'm developing more retention, danger danger, boil and bubble, trouble.

"... you must recall all the diseases. Is that what you want?"

"That is not it, that is not what I meant at all." Ellie felt her mind slipping free like a boat drifting from its mooring.

"You don't sound certain."

"Because it's so hard to explain." Ellie went to the controls, and surprisedly Joy let her work them. She turned time back on the screen and pointed, "You see here, 2002, it was still Old Way and I..." Ellie hesitated, cautious but she knew she had already gone too far to turn back, "I had a child. Lisa. In the Old way. Lisa was to-be-death."

Joy's entire body and mind seemed to squeeze itself into one single steel ball, "You remember Lisa?"

"She was...death. And I...hurt."

No. You can't possible remember pain! No one ever has."

"It was hurt, Joy, but not negative. The hurt was so much a part of the love that..." Ellie stopped mid-sentence, frozen by Joy's stilito stare. After a moment's pause, Ellie made an incredible thrust of perception, "...that it was as if..I liked hurt."

Even with her Ultimate Mechanics, Joy could not find a tool to hide her horror: "How did you remember that? And don't dare tell me you read it on the screen because I can feel you remembering a past experience."

"That's true. Ellie surrendered more information, "I know that the girl called Lisa was not my clone. She...I imagine, they have not even let you know this much, but she was inside me. Joy, we had...wombs."

Coldly Joy told her, "I know that. You forget I am Select. Allowed into the studies. But only Selects have the strength for negative information. You aren't able to hold such thoughts. You couldn't even live with the memory of the pain you think you remember as childbirth. No, nor could you really stand the thought of that inconceivable idea, to-be-death. We saved you from all that. How did you get hold of that negative thought?"

"I told you that other than that mishap with the computer, I don't know." Ellie thought, "I suppose there was some positive in the birth, so that even with the pain, the holding her and loving her led me to --" Ellie stopped again.

"Precisely." Joy hit the desk smiling now, "You are just what I always warned them about. You prove my theory. I have contended, argued at length, in fact, that if allowed any Retention, even apparent positives, the unselected will evoke their opposites from them. It was the same with the others."

"Others? How many? Are they chosen? Did they..."

"Do you hear how morbid you are becoming?"

"I'm not morbid. I only want to know."

"Want to know! For what reason? Everything is provided, what can that mean to you, 'Want to know'? Perhaps you've somehow become tired."

"How can I be tired? This body won't tire and you know it. Joy, have you ever heard the rumor---" Ellie paused, but then concluded she had nothing more to lose now, "---the rumor that we have a ---spiritual nature?"

"Not only have I never heard of such a thing, but I can't even conceive of a meaning for what you ask."

Ellie went on, "That there is something to us, other than our bodies. That we are more than we see?"

"Inconceivable."

"Will you at least hear me out?"

"You know I have to today, even if you're bizarre."

Ellie took rapid advantage: "Somewhere. Sometime. Even before my primary PCL, I read something. I suppose they thought it was too soon for me to have any comprehension, but anyway, it was a Plato, I remember that. Plato."

"A Plato. I don't recognize the thought."

"Well, I've read the definition."

Joy bites each word, "There is no such thing as a Plato."

"It's a name."

"I have never heard of anyone by that name."

"I know. We only kept the Aristotle. But there was a Plato. And a Socrates."

"You are doing a very dangerous thing, Ellie. You're inventing vocabulary."

"There were others, too, Joy. A Jesus. A Buddha. And evidently, much like them, a Shelley and a Bryon and Keats and two women, Emilies with wonderful minds that were not scientists."

"Absurd."

"They did something called religion. They played minds at something called philosophy and there were poetry and there were those, before the Development who thought there was a central creator..."

"Our Creator Corporation has never been hidden, Ellie. It always was, it is and always will be. Really, Ellie, where do you think your hearts and lungs and all your parts come from?"

"The Creator Corporation?"

"Right."

"But, Joy, have you never wondered where the Creator Corporation came from?"

"I have never heard such thoughts in my existence. The Creator Corporation has given you all things and---" Joy shook her head in obvious and real wonder, "You are having some of the strangest mental constructs I've ever come across in my time at FDO. I'm surprised you can even word such ideas. I'm afraid you are having some serious malfunctions."

"If that's the case, then you can consider---"

"No. You are not a MalFunct! It's only your brain that has some..."

"My mind!"

"Your brain! And that's the easiest equipment we fix. I think all you'll need is a little tuck in the left side."

"Did you know I once had another brain? That we come from clones with brains of flesh and that I only got this one in 2032?"

"Did you know that there is no such thing as flesh?"

"I had an original brain, Joy. We were flesh. Skin and all

those organs were real flesh that..."

"THAT is entirely enough, Ellie, this may be one of your Most Speical Days and because of that I have been inordinately patient but..."

"... and those bodies used to die, naturally. All of them. After a certain period of time, it just happened. They did not have to be eligible."

"Ransom!" Joy was a command such as Ellie had never heard, "I have never had to evoke Power. To my knowledge, Power has not been used, or necessary in over fifty years."

Ellie realized how long fifty years was, "In other words, there was no real question of eligibility, or getting the decision from FDO. All simply, naturally, died."

Oddly, Ellie suddenly knew that Joy's anger was born of fear, "It's true, Joy. One day, before Jubilation Week, I began memory for some reason. And talking about it finally makes me realize all the more. There were some people that had to-be-believe, and they thought that after the to-be-death, there was an afterdeathlife.

"I see. Obviously Ransom, there will have to be repairs. I'm not even sure if I can articulate your notions. There is life, and life and more life. That is all there is."

"Sometime, Joy, I have lately, a sense of before before. Before I was born. You see, I had parents, not just in-clone, but flesh. There was beyond matter, being. All sorts of things were there. Causes and effects until your mind got back to a First Thing, and then, there was ...mystery."

Imperceptible, as Ellie spoke the work, Joy hit the emergency button, saying, "Ransom, you are Product. You are a fortunate..."

"They had...blessing."

"...fortunate to be a Product One, a given. You are a simple creation of the Corporation."

"I'm sorry. I don't believe that is my original creation."

"Blasphemy." Joy could barely whisper her outrage but Ellie was not frightened. For some reason, the new horrible negative thoughts excited Ellie so that she wanted them to go on; new ideas grew from the previous ones and tumbled her mind: love to be or not to be, greater love hath none, a far far better thing than starry night madness requiems of Mozart flames of the maiden Joan all the horrors came wonderful; the mystery, oh, they even thought if they lived a certain way called a value they would reward.

"The Corporation gives every possible reward without your slightest effort." Abandoning pretense, Joy was openly reading Ellie now.

"For some reason I can't explain, Joy, that's not the same. They thought to --- earn. I think the word is earn --- to earn this heaven where there was only joy, no weeping or pain or sorrow or death."

"Fully circle. You describe your life on Cosmosterra just as the Corporation has given it to you."

Yes. Ellie saw how foolish the thought was. Joy was right of course. She should be completely satisfied. She had everything she could possibly want. Except one.

Ellie wanted to die.

Suicide was out the question except for the few Elite in the Construct and Destruct Departments of Bodily Equipment. Parts were indestructible and no one knew enough of their own composition to destroy it. So, Ellie almost laughed, they were condemned to perfection. Her thoughts tumbled again though she knew Joy was reading: love, cross sacrifice danger hero struggle conquest, that was it! There! Each negative did precisely birth a positive before the world according to skinner. Skinner? No, no, Ellie's mind was screaming to accept the happiness where a woman did not have to suffer the inexpressible pains of childbirth nor the loss of mother or a soldier and no fighting because the Corporation brought only joy on joy, cloned on and on and on in the continuum circle, ascending ascending and ascending, never a descent, only the one hand.

"You see?" Joy asked, and Ellie quickly responded, "Yes."

"It's all for the best." And again Ellie agreed in the positive.

"Now then, we can't clone you as you are because the renewed you would still have this inanity of wanting eligibility as well as that mental demon-brew you're making up. Poetry and mystery and this phenomenal idea that good can come from negative, which to my knowledge has never been thought before."

"Yes."

"It won't take five minutes."

"I volunteer." Ellie said as if there were a choice. Ellie followed Joy down the corridor: Goodbye Edgar Allan Poe, the possibility of a Plato, Nietzsche, da Vinci, Hitler, Goodbye Tolstoy, Anne Frank, Jesus, Attila, holocausts, Goodbye Emilies, Hegel, Lisa --- They were in front of the PCL Adjustment Lab; goodbye plagues and poem; goodbye time.

III

The perpetual early morning sun shone perfectly as Joy stood by the window of the FDO building just in time to see Robert and his wife Ellie jogging happily up the mountain, laughing.

The Disappearance of Davy Kramer

I

David Kramer always believed in Atlantis; that must be clearly understood or nothing wonderful can happen. Also, it needs to be mentioned at the onset, that for that very reason, Davy had always been the butt of jokes around McDowell County, West Virginia, as in, "Hey, let's get a six pack and go over to Davy's haunted house."

Now the joking has ended. Davy's gone.

To paraphrase Davy's view of what was going to happen, he would "achieve a calculated conceptual mental-emission that will allow me to transport myself from our too limited dimension."

To paraphrase our friends, "Davy's disappeared."

Of those friends, I was perhaps the last one to have seen Davy. As he grew more and more convinced of his radical ideas, friends came around less and less. I realize now, that that was his intention; for when he had completely finished his renovations, he could not have wanted many people to be there. Whatever his intent, friends came less and less to his alleged "haunted house".

I have lived in the small mountain town of Kimball, West Virginia, all my life. When Davy Kramer moved here in November of 1983, the town found it amusing at first, if incomprehensible. When he bought the old abandoned boardinghouse up Carswell Hollow, there was outright laughter. That was the period in which King Coal was reigning in McDowell County, creating a boom as the region was located in the very bowels of the Pocahontas Coal Seam. McDowell County, during this brief Camelot era, was a mecca for much of the world's unemployed.

But when King Coal was dethroned after World War II, the region returned to an all but inaccessible, seamy economically depressed district which became the front for President Johnson's War on Poverty.

During the heyday of the boardinghouse, rumors had it that Lena Roschella was a witch from the southern parts of Italy where the evil eye and other forms of sorceries were hatched. Stories were told saying that Lena had a family history in the old county that went all the way back to the Etruscans; that her family could be traced to before the Roman Empire, when in the mists of far times, those aborigines searched the entrails of animals for prophecies.

In fact, my own mother told me that Lena worked some magic with oil and water and that something in the swirl of the two fluids gave her powers to portend. But the most biting evidence was my niece, Rosemary. When she was an infant, she was ill to the point of death. Lena had done some still undefined magic with the oil and water that was supposed to cure her. Now I don't believe in such things; but then again, Rosemary is one of my favorite nieces, and still very much with us.

Whatever real powers lay in the head and heart and spirit of Lena Roschella were assumed to have died with her in 1949. From that time on, the huge eleven-room boardinghouse was empty, and to we children, of necessity in a town with less and less activity, haunted. During the next thirty years, the boardinghouse was reduced, by climate and vandals, to a near shell which we all assumed would dwindle down to wood that would become once more part of the mountainside. There were other odd objects that were expected, through the centuries, to sink into the earth and never be seen again.

Then Davis Kramer came to Kimball. He bought the boardinghouse and all of the land attached to it from the railroad company, which during the King Coal era owned most of the lands and all of the mountains around Kimball. Not exactly joining in the guffaws, I did smile with amusement when Davy told me, "I was drawn to this place. It's no accident, I'm here, Fran. I've been searching the world over since the 1960s looking for the spot, and now I've found it."

"The spot?" I looked at him, knowing everyone was beginning to assess him as harmless, but insane. What I saw was a well-dressed, highly-educated, articulate and jovial gentleman.

He was almost British in bearing; there were no signs of manic behavior, depression or anything in the least radical in his demeanor. He drove the previous year's model Volvo; apparently had advanced degrees and intended to get a teaching position in the local high school, though it was very evident that he was independently wealthy. I later learned that he did have degrees in English literature with minors in philosophy, though he preferred teaching history, in which he had advanced degrees. His favorite period, in which he had some sixty-odd hours, though not a PhD., was in ancient civilizations.

"You do know that this boardinghouse is in the eastern extremity of the coal seam, don't you?" Knowing about his education and interests, I did not react at the odd remark made some months after we had become acquainted. Davy added on that occasion, "Coal. You know, the underworld and all its myths. Natural resources and all the accompanying wealth. Pluto. Spiritual wealths as well."

Though I own and write the local newspaper, as an English major in college I had enough grounding in mythologies to follow most of Davy's references. As a matter of fact, after an esoteric period in the 1960s, I could understand the eastern allusions, so I just chalked it up to eccentricity and perhaps a little too much Edgar Allan Poe when he was younger. The latter conclusion was the result of both his statement and syntax when he talked about such things. For example, when Davy first told me of being drawn to the boardinghouse up Carswell Hollow, he said that he had pulled as if "from a force immanent in a maelstrom. I was literally sucked into this place."

Davy's joviality and hospitality made the place popular with friends at first, but as he began the extended renovations, and went more deeply into his subjective "maelstrom", fewer and fewer people were willing to venture into the building. Now, I assumed that was Davy's design all along.

I remained faithful, however; the dual lures of concern and fascination kept me with him. We confessed to each other our experiments with psychedelic drums in college; and, admittedly, I often wondered if some such source might not be fueling his contemporary life. Still, for an entire first year, I can't say I had any serious misgiving about what might occur in the old building.

But that house! Great Edgar Poe, what a place! For eight

months after many people had stopped visiting, the town of Kimball watched in astonishment as huge trucks came in, day after day, carrying all sorts of stones, cement mixers, etc. No one cared where Davy got the money for such reconstruction; all were too curious about the construction itself to think of anything else. But curiosity was thwarted before he began the actual work on the building. Davy built a thirty foot high wall, very much like some extravagant ediface around an ancient European castle. Incredibly, the wall enclosed parts of the Tug and Elkhorn rivers that forked on the end of Carswell Hollow.

Some locals were upset about what they felt was the confiscation of some of their natural rights; but, in fact, the deed from the N and S Railroad gave Davy all that territory where the rivers forked. This later proved to be another one of the reasons he was so sure he had found his "spot".

Months went by in which no one was allowed to go there. When I was finally invited to come to the boardinghouse upon its completion, I laughed when Davy gave me a map to get in. He seemed surprised by my laughter, "Fran, you will need this to get in. I've expanded the building into the side of the mountain. You won't recognize it as the place you once played as a child."

Then he had walked off leaving me holding the map, with only half a smile left on my face. Even the half-smile faded when I unfolded the map. Instead of the expected linear map; it was concentric:

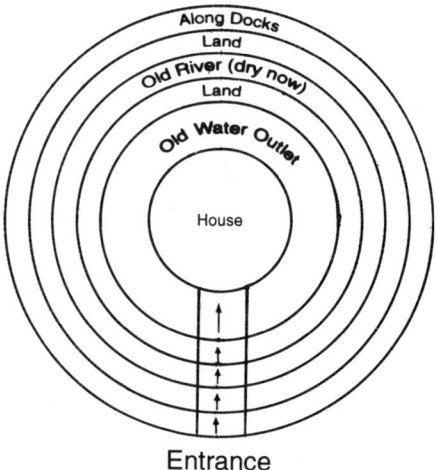

Amazingly, he had re-routed parts of the Tug and Elkhorn rivers as well as part of some of the small mountain streams and created in fact, a castle-with-moat concept. The boardinghouse itself was kept intact, though expanded into the mountainside as he had told me. Davy said he thought its prior usage was essential to his mission. Though intact, the renovations were astonishing; great oaken wood floors; marble mantlepieces, candleabra, etc., made the place a mansion.

Realizing he must be a closet millionaire, I was speechless, but Davy seemed to find my amazement disconcerting and wanted to know what was wrong. When I muttered something to the effect of never expecting to see a mansion in McDowell County, Davy grew irritable, saying that he thought I was someone who could understand.

The only comment I could think of immediately was, "Well, Davy, this place of yours is certainly a marvel."

"It is not 'my place', Fran, I'm only a tenant here." Leading me back across the room which was furnished in Victorian fashion so that I felt I was being pulled across a room on Baker Street, Davy sat me back in a high-backed chair. It was readily apparent that I was someone he trusted; that realization created a maternal feeling in me and I tried to be open to his enthusiasm when he asked me what I had been thinking.

"Actually, I was thinking of about forty-five ways to kill you..." There was no reaction at all in the beautiful dark eyes, "... and hide your body in all the mud caked on my fifty dollar shoes."

"Oh that." Davy dismissed my remark; he would not be distracted, "But did you realize when you approached over the bridge that you were walking along a long lost altered waterway? That there had in fact been actual larger bodies of water in this region that a cataclysm may have created these very Appalachian Mountains as well as other major North American contemporary topological regions."

That was the first moment when I became seriously concerned, "Davy, I don't think..."

"This was a major port. The canal outline, that's all I could really reconstruct, of course, only the outline of the canal in the original design, you do recognize the design – from Plato's description of Atlantis."

"Really, Davy." I looked around, "This is really getting out of hand. The town talks about you..."

"That I'm insane, ok." He rushed to the fireplace, picked up a fire iron which evidently was a remote because as Davy lifted it, the mantle turned around and exposed a safe. "I'm going to show you something, Franny." He then opened the safe and took out a brown crumpled piece of paper: "I found this in what must have been the old woman's wine cellar." He carefully unfolded the paper which threatened to disintegrate as quickly as some long sealed contents of an ancient pharaoh's tomb. I looked down on:

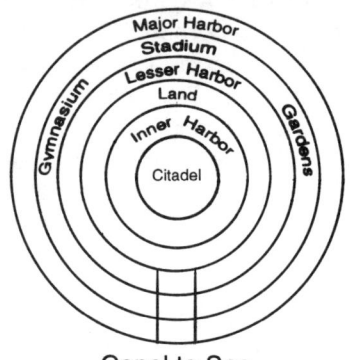

On beneath the map was written:

Lena Pesapina Roschella

1282 AD

II

Whatever initial feelings of humor or interest I had originally held were now submerged in apprehensions about Davy's consummate passion. He no longer made a pretense of teaching; resigned that position and now spent every waking hour reading books of an esoteric nature, particularly Blavatsky's **Isis Unveiled**, Alistair Crowley, general mysticism and meditation. Needless to say, he could not find most of his books in the McDowell County Library, so he had huge orders of boxed books coming to the Kimball Post Office two or three days a week. The oddities were well known as, unfortunately Davy had gone in and asked for Madame Blavatsky's works; and the boxes which came to the town's post office were certainly from companies that generally did not deliver there: Zarathustra's Press; The Inner Eye Vision; Maharishi Krishnamurta Newsletter: Hyperion Now News: Icarus' Landing Press, etc.

Post mistress Tina Green (who in fact scanned some of the material that was not hermetically sealed) said after the disappearance: "I knew it, I just knew it."

So did I. As the only person now allowed entrance to the boardinghouse, I knew that after the first eight months of intense singular study; Davy began his experiements. As in Poe, all of Davy's other "friends had flown before", making my connection with him all the more important. However, for a period of four weeks, even I was not allowed to see him; he paid young Zachary Green to deliver books, food, and any other necessaries. Then, after a month of complete isolation, I received a call asking me to come to visit him. Though I knew he did not want to hear about it; I could not help but comment on his disshelved appearance. He was gaunt, haggard and thinning to the point that seemed both unattractive and unhealthy.

He ignored my concerns entirely, "Fran, this is it! I'm reaching, what shall I call this point, not an idea, no, not thought, more feeling, I guess, yes, I feel, feel that I am reaching what I've searched for all my life."

In spite of my fears for him, the rambling fractured syntax, the rush of excitement that he conveyed transmitted like an electrical charge into me. He stood there with an intensity of expression on his face that screamed for a Rodin to mold it to immortality. His determination and certainty conceived in me an odd openness to his expression, though I felt foolish about the same. I did realize it was important to him to have someone say to him, "I'm not laughing, Davy."

"I knew you wouldn't. And that is vital to me."

"I see that now. But though I'm not laughing, Davy, I have to tell you I'm not happy about what's going on here. Not that I know what that is."

My reservations had no more impact than did a full town's laughter; he began to pace, explaining: "It's as if I've spent my whole life climbing up a mountain, and now, on the brink, on its precipice I am being pulled down, into eternity."

I did not like the sound of that at all; but, being the only person with whom he would communicate, I used caution in stating reservations. "Davy, I was wondering if I might get you away from here for just a few hours. Maybe go to dinner."

"Fran, you don't understand the nature of what I've discovered. We none of us can ever truly experience another's experiences." As always, he gave me much to think about as he went on, "So, it stands to reason that you cannot really assimilate, or incorporate as your own, my experiences, if they are not part of your own. And if you have no true virtual experience of my experience, how can you evaluate it?"

During the silence and space he gave me to think in, the only response I could make was that, for the sake of a society's continuance, one must conclude that if only one person maintained the veracity of a certain experience, then it must be assumed to be faulty. Without even uttering it, I knew his refutations: the rarity of the event did not negate its veracity; besides which, the psychic, phenomenological and miraculous experiences had an unknown number of participants which the contemporary sciences had spent considerable time, monies and talents to discredit.

But a strong, faithful, residue of advocates remained and though all did not have the resources to create the system of verification that the Edgar Cayce Foundation commanded; they did have volumes of evidence for unexplained actualities. I determined to listen non-critically: "I'm listening."

He breathed a sign of relief: "Good. It is important that I leave a record behind." I did not indicate the chill that statement evoked; he continued, "I think---feel, whatever preference of terminology is comfortable to you, that I have reached a position of unique transcendence."

"I don't follow, Davy. When I first met you, you were not in the least religious. You demanded that the rational be the criteria..."

"You see, don't you Franny, that's your problem. The problem of the whole huge hulk of humanity at the moment." He spoke with such sadness that I overlooked the fact that he was being somewhat insulting, "The conclusion seems to be that one cannot be both religious---spiritual, and rational. As a species anymore, most of us won't see the forest for the trees. Worse, we're cutting down the forests looking for the trees."

I stated what to me was a cliché, "You're simply saying that we stayed so steeped in the physical that we aren't cognizant of our spiritual natures."

"Too precise. And even if it is a cliché..." That was the first indication I had that he was reading my thoughts, "We still keep driving those interstates that take us outward, when in fact, we need to travel within."

"The locale of the kingdom."

"Yes. As well as the prime tenets of most faiths. And the more secular, like Socrates. Know Thyself. Elementary philosophy; thoughts from the first dawn of thought, and still we have not incorporated it." It seemed best to make no comments, but just listen to the verbal flow: "And Plato even more. And Pythgorus even more than both. That long ago, they knew we were without boundaries. We are, in fact, bound, limited only because of, and to the degree that we believe we are bound, limited. You see, the very reason that you say something to me such as --- you thought me rational rather than religious, is because you have me categorized. Compartmentized. Aristotle and all those sciences that think they know and never pause to know that they do not, that's the problem. And the Twentieth Century has completed that damage; if our scientists cannot measure, understand or explain something, the conclusion is that the unexplained reality is not real. We never see the whole. Only pieces and parts and we buy every piece and part they make because we Madison-Avenue, mind-controlled Westerns are the most sad ever."

The amount of wonderful ideas sandwiched between the statements of utter madness astounded me. But when he paused, I knew he wanted me to say something. I had not stopped him; firstly, because I was fascinated by what he was saying, and secondly, I felt he was at some risk and it necessitated my having as much understanding of him as I could. Pressed to say something germane to his statement, I was inane: "Sounds like you've been reading up on Hinduism."

I could all but feel the pain that he felt: "More category. It's not your fault; it's a well we are sunken in. It's not Hindu or Buddhist or Jain, but All. That's what I'm talking about, the All. It's beyond any Book, beyond any idea that separates. You see, Fran, I've begun the real trip Within. I am becoming my Idea. Me."

Oh God! I had almost cried out, but was able to suppress it. I have loved him, been amused, interested in all the things he did, but now I knew his sanity was at stake. If I had any doubts left, he confirmed my fears with his next statement: "I dissolved a tree yesterday."

"Dissolved, Davy, you dissolved a tree."

"I brought it right back, you know me better than that."

"Davy, listen to me..."

"You listen. You'll marvel. This phase began gradually, of course. It's as Alan Watts says, time is no measure for the coming of the realization to anyone. A person might spend a lifetime striving toward it, and never achieve it. Then another might just glance away from a play at a ball game, and it comes to him in a flash. It can, you know, come for some, without their conscious effort. Those, however are the ones who often don't realize what has occurred."

"Nirvana, I guess."

"If you have to name the unnamable, Nirvana is as good as any word." I could not help but be absorbed, and once again I abandoned apprehensions and listened, "All this..." his arms swept pointedly around the paraphenalia of the room, "All of this, this unfeeling, unseeing matter that we accept day after day as our reality, that we've learned to measure our identity by accumulating, is meaningless. And it's obtuse meaninglessness is the major obstacle between our distinguishing between the unreal and the Real."

He stopped, deep in thought so I asked, "Davy, on the phone, you said something about this being the beginning. The beginning of what?"

"I'm not certain." And that was the first indication I had of Davy's own apprehension as he sat, dejected, "I really don't know."

I hated to see him so down, so, despite that fact that I felt I shouldn't encourage him in this pursuit, I did ask him to try to explain at least what he meant by "the beginning". I immediately regretted making the request, because it obviously plunged him down to a new depth of depression, "Even that is difficult. See, I'm too much the product of Western empirical teaching to be open to the vast potentiality of the All. I've been too long impressed, and I mean that precisely. My mind and soul with all their forms of separations and fragmentations clog my inner eye."

"Davy, I have to tell you I'm concerned by what you call the dissolving of that tree."

"Seems far out, huh? But it's so simple. With all the religious rhetoric that flies around, we don't realize how absolute, how total, the power of faith is. Jesus, nor any of the prophets spoke idly when they spoke of the ability to move mountains. You note scripture, with each miracle he places the companion comment, "If you truly believe". We pass over such things, not allowing their truth; trusting matter as the only reality. Perhaps Berkeley at least had some clue."

Once more, Davy slipped into the absurd as if it were the ordinary. My mind calculated: perhaps he was too isolated here; saw no one but me, and that less and less frequently, and he never left the place. Davy became aware of my distraction and then began a new unusual phase; from that point on, he spoke in the plural. "Soon after we initiated the advance meditations, we realized that we were beginning a not unprecedented, but most assuredly, a unique level. How can we describe that which is beyond description." He was pacing around the room now, "There's nothing we can relate in recorded history because the nature of it is beyond recording. We assume it to be beyond beyond. What we can say, is that it implements, or includes, yes, includes is the better term, includes union, harmony, peace and a selflessness..." His face lit up. I knew he had found an agreeable form of expression, "Do you know Eliot? The term in "The Wasteland?"

I immediately recognized the reference, "Shantih?"

"Shantih." He savored the word, "The peace beyond understanding."

Though the suggestion was inane, I was now frightened by the sound of his voice, pleasing on one level; on another, he seemed literally eons back in time, so I suggested we go to see "Evita". Foolishly, I even tried to talk about the new spiritual direction Madonna was taking; his look of pity silenced me. "Fran, I believe I may have seen the origin."

"Origin? Of what?"

He seemed to find that question as foolish as the suggestion that we go to a movie, "The Origin. How feeble are words as a vehicle of communication. What we lost when we lost the telepathic path. We have lost so much of what we had. We once knew, were one, in Creation, love and union. Plato is precise." His face clouded, "But we surrender to Conflict, chaos, division and then this gross individualization. Separation is the cause of earth, matter."

Separation is the cause of earth. Admittedly, even that point there were still moments when I all but envied him. Perhaps he was insane, but then again, perhaps this was utter sanity: separation is the cause of earth. There was such a sadness in his voice for all of us as he spoke that it evoked the headlines; Rwanda, Eastern Europe, Hebron, the beautiful Ramsey child slain with the unutterable accusations: "Division became individualization, the Eye was lost to the gross I, my need, my greed into the hard distinct definite concepts of Self against other Selves. And yet, even in the growing distinctions, the immortal memory of our Ideal past remains, the yearning to come together, to rise above our Self. That yearning, the real but lost root of sexuality that seeks to Unite but has been reduced to the lowest common practice, the search for the Perfect Orgasm."

"And that explains for you, the separation of you and I and others in the latter day Twentieth Century?"

"In part it does. And Sartre is correct when he says, that in the frame of that type Self, Hell is others. But he concludes for the wrong reasons. It's not the existence of others that accounts for torment, but the separation of Self into selves."

"I doubt you could convince Sartre."

"There's the beauty. I don't need to convince anyone anymore."

"Ha, that sounds like paradise enou."

"It is, Franny, it is."

The moment seemed a conclusion; I certainly had nothing else to say so I left. Needless to say, left with mixed emotions. Fog from Kell's Mountain was pouring over Davy's wonderfully created moat as I left the boardinghouse; I had a sense of utter displacement. I thought about going to the movie alone, but the idea of that pretense seemed wholly unattractive. I went home.

III

For the next two months, I heard nothing more from Davy. I could not contact him as his phone and computer were both disconnected and the idea of going to the boardinghouse uninvited was out of the question. Most days, from my window at the *Kimball Weekly News*, I watched as Heath and Zachary Green delivered food; there was no longer any mail; books were no longer necessary to Davy Kramer. As the hot August sun thrust its heated head into our office, my reporter, Brandon Dorcas decided he would like to do a feature on the condition of the county since Johnson's Great Society waged its war against those conditions. Our small papers often received grants for such programs so Brandon and I went to Washington to work on the report. I invited the immersing of myself in the fantasies of this world and its power, fully intending to obliterate the possibilities Davy had suggested.

When Brandon and I returned to Kimball, I learned that Davy had called the office while I was away. Apparently, from a pay phone so I had no way to call back. I decided to leave a note with the Greens' groceries and I received a note back asking me to come to the boardinghouse the next night. Though nothing surprised me any more, I did note the oddity; instead of meeting inside, he wanted to meet in the area where the inner waterway had been reconstructed. Overcoming my thought of the sludge I would have to dredge through, and dressing rattily for that reason, I went to the suggested spot.

The irritation I felt with myself for responding immediately any time he called, vanished when I saw his emaciated face. It was dusk and what little sunlight remained crept through the sky spraying dimly down into the bog created by his reconstruction and innovations. I had to remind myself I was meeting an old friend of some fifteen years now and that nothing omnious was going to happen.

Davy's condition was what I wanted to talk about first; he dismissed those comments with a statement to the effect that fasting was essential, and that if I wished to help him, I must ignore such material visuals either in his being or his belongings. Because?

"Fran, I am at the end of the beginning."

I would call Dr. Mariana Linz, a psychologist friend as soon as I left him this evening. The stench of the sludge he had created was all too materially and aromatically real for me. I knew now, as I should have known previously, that professional help was necessary, but I also knew that I would need information that he might not give Dr. Linz, "Davy, why did we meet out here?"

"Please forget the trivial. Overcome your Self for the moment, please Fran. If you will, you may begin to overcome it entirely. Go beyond that body and dissolve your material entity toward All."

I could not imagine a link he retained with reality. Though his manner was sure and calm and he spoke gently, I knew that could not be the case. I was beginning to tire of the situation. While in D.C., I had contracted to do a book about the country from 1967-1997 and I was very excited about that reality. Yet, the truth remained, that I was Davy's only personal outlet, "Davy, listen to me. I think you're getting a little too carried away with this..." I searched for the word, "...study. I've known people into meditation and I've heard claims about out-of-body experiences..."

I was not saying what I meant to say and he looked painfully sad, "You really can't understand either. We're beyond that. We're completely immersed, or have been for the short periods of time we've been allowed in-state. Can you understand that during those times, I have been utterly without Being."

"Well, Davy, you sure as hell are standing here in front of me right now. At least, what's left of you." Speaking so, a chill ran through me, the feeling getting stronger and stronger. Night lay dismally dark around the place now as if Lena's boardinghouse itself were brooding. I looked around for some small glimmer of light; but knew without him speaking it, that Davy thought himself beyond electricity; that he had no need for artificial light.

"Don't be afraid, Fran. Life is such a short ephemeral contingency to your true existence. I only wish you peace, surely you know there's no harm here. It's only frightening to your because it's unknown to you."

In spite of my rational evaluations, Davy's voice brought an unwarranted relief. I grew calm as he told me that through meditation and contact with All, he had learned to displace his position in our Era, or Time. That space and distance had been consumed in Hereness; that all he need do now was to reach that totality again, work to sustain it, and he would enter forever there beyond measures of time or space."

"Davy, I don't think..."

"Rational argument is like sand, you sink in it. You may have had these experiences yourself and dismissed them. You were going to tell me you never heard of such a thing. There are historical accounts. Oriano Monannini disappeared in Tuscany in 1378. During the Medieval era, in Lyon, Guy Villete disappeared and both those recorded exits were from churches where every exit was watched. They did not leave by physical exits, Fran. We know they were transported."

"I doubt such esoteric heights can happen in West Virginia in 1997, Davy."

"Facetiousness belittles us both right now."

"You're right and I'm sorry. But I'm also concerned at what's happening to you. There could be a dozen other explanations for what you're experiencing."

"I suppose. For those who find it necessary to find other explanations. But then I need to remind you, that among those explanations is the fact that we have entered the State we described. And that others have gone before."

"Davy, no."

"I'm going tonight, Fran. I only can hope someday you'll follow."

Like hell! I stopped talking to him, planning how I would describe the conversation to Dr. Linz. But, instead of leaving him immediately as I intended, I began to walk around the rooms of the boardinghouse. I found, that Davy had made plans to prove whatever he planned to do. Every doorway, except the one we had entered was cemented closed. When I found the first one, I turned to look at him: "Go on. Go over the entire building. The basement, the side doors, the backdoor, there is no exit or entrance other than the one we came in.

It now entered my mind, that the whole thing was a hoax. Davy was not only sane, buy zany. He intended to leave and create some sort of legend, not all that unlike the one Lena Roschella left behind. I decided to play the game; but seriously, "If you are serious, I want you to let me bring Brandon here and check these doors."

Though it was impossible for this man to now hide his disappointment in me; I admit to a fleeting moment of appraisal his extraordinary purity. He agreed, and when I came back to the boardinghouse with Brandon we searched a full four hours, every nook and cranny of Lena's building: completed sealed and cemented closed, except the one entrance. I told Brandon only that it had to do with a magician's trick that Davy was doing; he believed that, as in fact, in part it was the truth.

By this time, it was nearly 2 a.m. Brandon and I stationed ourselves at the entrance, intending to make sure that if one dropped off to sleep the other would be awake. It had not been necessary as Brandon was now almost as caught up in the intrigue as I was.

The reader knows the outcome of course. It would be mine if I were reading instead of experiencing the story. At the first spray of dawn's early light Brandon and I entered the room. David Kramer was gone.

Determined that we discover the hoax, we again spent most of four hours searching the boardinghouse. David Kramer had disappeared.

Remaining there so he could not sneak out, I sent Brandon to get the police and when they came to the house, I suggested that I suspected foul play, thus insuring that their search would be all the more thorough. No Davy. For the next month and a half, I hired professional detectives to search for him; with the Internet and other modern modalities of discovery, I was sure, if he was anywhere, he'd be found.

Nowhere. He had not left Carswell Hollow. He had not caught any means of transit out of the region, none that were known to transport physical bodies through space.

IV

I picked up the ringing phone, "Can you come over?"

"Davy!" I screamed and ran to my car. As soon as I entered his study I shouted at him, "Where have you been?" I was all but hysterical; he was tranquil and that infuriated me, "Davy, that was not funny."

"Fran, I am not joking."

"Where have you been?"

"Exactly where I told you I'd be."

I settled into the chair, very tired. He was not going to change his story and I could not prove it untrue. He began to explain: "There are bodhisattvas. I come back this once. To have you know, Franny. As I started across the beautiful calm lake, though of course it was not in fact a lake, but I still maintained enough of my concrete soul to have to give it physicality. At any rate, a scent arose, as if the we were lying inside the petals of all the flowers in the universe and we were gliding, so much in ecstasy that we trambled---that was it, of course."

"That was it?"

"Yes, the trembling, the experiencing on that level was a defect in spiritual transportation. We trembled because the trip felt to be taking so long---oh, there was the flaw, I'd kept some sense of time, so we realized that our preparation was not quite complete. So, we're here today for the final preparation."

"Now, Davy, you were not here. We searched the whole place."

"Of course I was not here. You're still thinking in terms of time and space."

To hell with it! I grabbed my coat and started to leave, but he reached out and touched me, "I had hoped you might come. But I can't wait. Shantih, Fran, shantih."

I pulled my arm away, furious, confused and disturbed: where had he been?

V

For five more months, though I never returned, I knew he was planning, praying, studying and fasting. Then, one morning in January, when the mountains were tall white heaps of snow, I found a note, "We transport tomorrow night."

I refused to be drawn in again but I did send Brandon and the Green boys to watch the exit. Davy did not leave. The next morning, I again joined them and the police in the search. Davy was not inside the boardinghouse.

Because of my position in the community, my profession and similar considerations, I did not say anything, nor write about it. But for the past year I have thought about the man in Tuscany and the one in Lyon; had they too had friends who would not speak out from various real or social fears?

I went to the boardinghouse and walked around; I was considering writing about it. That was when I received a message from Davy. I had gone there one afternoon, sad, wearied from the world's daily news. Whatever the reason, I felt the need for Atlantisian possibilities. I walked into his room and picked up a book at ransom. It was entitled Oriental Mysticism, but when I opened the book, all the pages were blank. I stood there, hypnotically transfixed that the published work of one Lin Sing Tui was only these fine blank pages. But as I stared at the pure immaculate pages, I began to feel that there had once been ebony letters, words across them, erased, and a sense of infinite peace filled me.

Then, slowly, imperceptibly, a movement began, so slow as if it were not taking place in time; a movement without movement, slowly, slowly, letter by letter, filling every page before me.

SHANTIH

Outre Montani

Medi-celestial
❋

Over the river a dark dank fog spreads upward.
It is the year 1347, Annos Domini.
The fog hovers.
Then begins to spread itself as if it is guided by some other intelligence; as if it is moving in accordance with some clear pre-destined Intent.

The fog meanders in dark shadows crawling up passed Gray Monk's Cathedral; passed the pillories. The fog moves like a silent song along the drawbridge. It stops. It scans the moat of the castle and then slowly climbs up the castle wall and enters it like a cold deathgas.

Through the stone crevices, down the dim halls and into the cell, the fog.

Every night now this same dream.

**

I feel strange.
I am in the cell. I feel myself in this cell.
Yet I did not come here by the drawbridge. And I did not come along the odd high roads that surround this unknown town. And I did not enter through the doors to this place.
I am here, but I did not come here.
I am located high in their tower; I know this.
Yet I did not climb up here.

I am free. I know this.
Yet, I am imprisoned.

I know that if I were allowed to leave I would not go. But I am not so allowed.

I would not know where to go now if I were to leave for I

know no roads outside; I cannot dream what paths or hallways, what damp alleys or what forests might lie outside this cell.
I do not know if there is anything outside this cell.
I come to think this may be All-Space; All-Time.

And I can only be here, in this place, for eternity.

I will never know another place and as I look about now I see there a body standing by the crack in the cell wall. The body has eyes; I think that is what they call those apertures, eyes, and with these, looks out of the crack in the wall and watches the fog outside.

I am hovering near that body.
Again, this strangeness comes on me; the sense of being alien becomes stronger and stronger the nearer I approach the

Body!!!
Helion Hellllliiiiiiiioooonnnnnn!!

I. It is me. I am entering the body in the cell again; I am returning once more, I am becoming body again, Oh Helion, No no no! falling, falling falling, down down returning returning turn turn turning and

Longing returns.
The first thing to turn me back again, is the longing. There, near the center of my body, there it rises, the longing.
Can this be? Can it be me feeling feeling? Longing? I?
Hunger.
That is the word they have when they talk of this longing in the center of the body. Hunger. I. Me. I hunger. That is their earthen name for the fallacy; hunger, and now I know it.
I am turned to Body again; Body I-am, and the dreary heavy weariness comes on me. It is, I am --- sleep.

***

"Eh, hey hey, you."
The clamorous screaming and beating at the door wakes me abruptly. I watch the door of the cell where each loud call is accompanied with a bang that shakes the wormy wood, "Eh,

you, ya hear me!"

What can this be? What comes now? What happens to me; I do not recall.

Me?

To a Me? What is a Me? Who am I and how do I come to be in this place, in this odd space that is so placeless?

But I am here. Now. For I experience. I hear the shout. What can THEY mean to me now? Still more punishment?

Please no. Surely this is enough. Even now, I hunger. I weary and I am allowed no rest; what more can they make me suffer?

"Wg eh ha!" The banging goes on; the sounds the entity makes are not all distinguishable for me. Yet, it goes on and on. So loudly. Sounds that in my Body-ears are massive dull cymbals that clanged down the corridor of time to fill the narrow space that is my single cell here now.

Ah Helion, why, why?

Helion?

What is Helion? Who? The other space; the other time when I

I? Who? Oh, Helion, the head of this body aches so. Helion again? Why this thought, Helion? What is the name and why does it come always to me? And what is this door and what is the thing outside that shouts and grossly bangs to enter instead of simply coming through the door.

No!

Of course. It cannot simply come through the wormy wood; it is too gross, too material, it cannot pass. And too, I am who I-am, and so it cannot enter without my volition.

But why? Who am I in that other space?

The Power.

I have the Power. Still. They cannot take that from me, whatever else. And the thing that bangs and shakes the wormwood door is of no avail against me. Only I can push the door open for him now. This time.

Each time.

For I am my prisoner.

****

The body begins to move across the cell; it falters, hesitates, unsure of the necessary movement of feet. A hacking cough begins in the cold lungs of the body and it goes on until the body can hardly breath. It sneezes and finally the unsavory mucus pours from its nostrils. It has never sustained, in memory, such physicality before. Discomfort permeates it; there is nothing to wipe the ooze with. It uses the sleeve of the odd covering of the arm and then feels the disgust of the cold sticky feeling coming through the sleeve and touching the skin.

The banging and shouting continues; I rise and go toward the door, shakily on the untried legs. Or should I say, the body starts across the cell, for I am not, can not be body.
 Yet, of course, I must be. I am body. The confusion again; it is not the body that I watch cross the cell, it is me crossing, the body and I are now some how, one. The arms and legs that feel the pain, feel the cold as if they had lain for ages in this self-same freezing water cell, is I-am.
 Power wanes.

I am across the cell, opening the gargantuan leaden door. I need no force to do so yet. I can still open it by thought for THEY, whoever they are for I do not remember Them except through a fog-of-mind. THEY cannot completely take Power from me. Though THEY can diminish them.
 As the door opens the eyes of the boy, my eyes sting with the sight of the fiery fragments from a single lantern that the banging being holds in its hands. In my dungeony place there now comes this one whose nature is barely above that of beast, and I must suffer it.
 The realizations of my dawning physicality are small discomforts compared to the horrendous hateful shattering of my sensibilities when I see the great fearsome gawky hairy entity. Before me it stands. It is long of height and a great heft of weight, so heavy that its bulk is difficult for me to focus upon. My eyes are drawn to its large protruding middle that looks as if a good sized boulder had been placed there and that someone had stretched skin, then cloth over it.
 At first I thought that it did not have speech as it did not say words that I could distinguish; more gross grunt than lyric. Nonetheless, this "Eh, hey, hey", meant something specific to it

and suggested at least a gutter utterance of a fractionally elevated beast. Though it is rudimentary in its elementary attempt at communication, there is little else about it that I recognize as being. Still, I feel it wishes to ask if there is an occupant in the cell; I discern from its small organ, they call it brain.

As I begin reading this brain-thing, Great Yeus!, it is aswirl with fears and distortions. What can cause such conditions in these creatures, if indeed they are creatures?

I feel for him, a pity. I want to ease him, to say to him, Know Thyself, but such ideas could not penetrate the gross brain-thing. So primitive. All his care and fear seems to be for that rude body that contains him. Odd. They seem to love those great senseless bulks. He loves it so that that great pulse-organ over the boulder of that belly is in great danger.

Great Yeus! I must act quickly or it will end its own entity with the fear. Somewhere still I remember that these beings end for some inexplicable reason when that great pulse-organ stops. Ah, there is their word; heart.

Quick now. I must slow it, slow slow, steady now, I mind him, I will slow that beat, calm the being, I will calm him; but even as I concentrate Power, the body bulk shakes before me. I begin searching mind to see if it does not have any form of communication but that most elementary, verbal language. Finally, I form from its own primitive TimeSpace oddity the speak: "Do not be afraid. There is no reason for fear. Fear is often no more than fear of itself. I think your types will come in later times to form such words as your own."

But at these calming words, it only quakes all the more and starts stammering, "No, no, no, ain't nobody in this cell. Ain't no Christian soul been in this cell, this canna be, I tell ya."

Only then do I realize my circumstance and know that I must quickly reconstruct an entire temporal-spatial mentality; for then is now to me; now is then.

How?

I don't know. That is not correct. It is not that I don't know; I don't remember. I must accept this now in order to survive; I must assume a physicality that will give me acceptability in their unusual constructs. I must become man as they are; must make the I-am that has a border, that suggests category and structure they call the-human, that is temporal and attached to bulk. I must border Being; exit my past; I must limit, and define the limit as to the creatures.

But why? Why? Why must I synchronize into conformity from my endowed formlessness? This I can not remember. I have spent eons elsewhere. I have moved forward, continuum by continuum, beyond all form, and now this.

And even as I try to select from the various conceptual structuralizations of my recent experiences, the fog, the cell, my assumption into flesh, the creature's quaking became inward and end-ward and I feel the sad burden of bulk fearing I will somehow end him. Sensing his senses, I rove memory of the rise of anger in these near-beasts, fled from time to the period of these ignorances, fears and hostilities and I
    still
    pity him,
Oh Helion! I still pity them.

*****

NO NO NO.

SOMETHING is screaming inside the Me; NO NO NO, Not again.

And yet, despite Memory: I pitied them.

Its pulse-organ is about to burst, so though I know the risk of Crossing Power and bringing it to beasties of the HereNow, I do so. Again. I raise thought and suspend the pulse-organ inside its body; I suspend all its processes; it is immobile.

Leaving it suspended in this state I begin the mental construct of its HereNow: I must do this so that I can translate them into some conceptualization that I will find workable. I find this:

1. Species: homosapien. (misnomer)
2. Galaxation positioning: eartheus.
3. Temporal positioning: circa the era their masters will later give the nomenclature, Annos Domini, year of Their Lord, some centuries following their Myth of the Nail.
4. General psychological conditioning; apparent indigenous ignorance of extemporality or exphysicality; fixative mentality; somewhat genital and culinary.

The period he was stationed in was one designate: Middle, Medieval, Dark Ages, Age of Faith; largely dormant productivity other than primitive agriculture; a redundance through several centuries of spiritual retardation; retaining many primitive concepts they accept, considered revelatory; cannibalistic communions were the commonplace; cross-sacrifice of one of their species became worthy of worship; they are subject to great demonical fears and illusionary impressions. Most of their fears are related to ---

Terminal!

Of course. Why didn't I recall that immediately. Great Yeus, of course. How could I have misplaced such a peculiar situation; these beings believe themselves only the-body, and so, terminal. Therefore, the entire mental construct is dominated by the idea of Nihil.

That is why they maintain the psychosis of the faith of the Nail; that is their only idea of the hope to be made non-terminal. What a curious reality level. Still, there is a pleasantness to the idea; the sleep; to have a time of consciouslessness as their later bard would write, "to shuffle off their mortal coil" must at times seem temptation: THEY could not imagine such a suspension.

But this is pedestrian thought and I have no time for it; I keep forgetting temporality. I must continue to construct critically. Apparently, in the Medieval Time there was a continent, Erpe. Spelled differently, but they separate into so many of the languages that it's hard to discern. This Erpe was taken from another myth, earlier than The Nail. One of their dawn-gods, a gross concept of diety named so close, Zeus, chased choice fleshy female mortal morsels (even now I fall into their alliterative forms; one of their few pleasantries), Europe, ah, Europa, there is the word.

This was part of a childish, though occasionally insightful set of mythologies that apparently diverted them from the idea of being terminal in that they thought the deities immortal. It seems they would later debunk these truths, never knowing how close they were moving to understanding.

But I am digressing; my mind is becoming like their's now, it wavers, falters, fails. Again, I garner facts: there is a continent of Europe and this planet Earth. The continent was rather small, irregular, a poorly conceived region, but even so it was surely wasted on such creatures that were evolving there.

They were all body-bound, like the flesh mound frozen before me now. Given to all sorts of ills and aches; imagined and real; given to decays and delusion behind what they are wont to call "reality". They are pest and plague-ridden, prone to slovenly anarchy; beings on whom Arthurian legends of Camelots must come again and again to alleviate their actualities.

So why, living in those wretched bodies, maimed as they are with those inconsequential minds, do they want to continue? Ah, yes, because they dare to delve into dream. Oh Helion, what I remember: they aspire.

I feel once more the sadness scream in me for these puppies of creation, these "creatures of a day". I begin to wonder about them; what is to come of all their futility, why are they here? The only way I can learn is to release this bulk before me; study his cause or effect and see if I can learn also how, why I am come among them.

I begin to release him from the suspension, slowly. Though primal, I will learn his sounds and try to understand his logic. Rudimentary though the words are, they do suffice enough to sustain their line of thinking, as I recall. But not very well. Later, they will have numerous self-annihilating holocausts. This among entities that so fear the Nihil even while they are its chief advocate.

Holocaust. I pause the Power a moment to wonder: how can these cretins ever reach a point where they conceived holocaust? They only barely know how to cause some light nights with these small crude insufficient fires, so how will they learn that totality?

Something taught them.

Some ----- thing-----.

Hurriedly now, I bring the thing back; I soothed its pulse-organ, heart and collateral activities, and returned it. As it comes back, it mutters some odd gasp: Holymotherogod!

"Who?"

"Jesus?"

"Who?"

"MOWTRY----MOWTRY", it begins to shout a confusing sound which I presume to be some sort of nomenclature for a comrade that he wants to startle badly. There is some mountain fearfulness in his shout: "MOWTRY!"

There was a grief of panic and I seek to ease it, having found their words: "It will be better if you calm yourself, sir. I will not suspend you again, I only did so to ease your heart, you see. You were in grave danger. There was no malintent on my part."

My attempt to placate him only appears to upset him the more, and incredibly, anger rises inside me and for a moment I was pleased to allow the emotion to dominate me as I could not recall feeling anything so strongly before. It is a curious feeling; a rising in the blood, a stirring and then it feels to grow heavier actually tingling the skin; sad to say, I believe I enjoyed it.

"Mowtry." He calls out again, but his voice and energies dissipate so that it is not a strong outburst this time. But unbelievably, at his call the emotion took over the body I-am and I shouted, "Shut up, idiot! You dolt! Have you no comprehension?" And I found myself ready to thrust the full Power on him, only to find my powers also dissipating. I-am diminishing. I try to go within again; nothing. Great Yeus, I am totally HereNow. I grow down to this one trembling before me.

I now too am only the victim-sailor in the sea of circumstance over which I have no control.

Then the Mowtry bursts into the room; another burley mass of brute strength. He runs across the dark cell, his keys jangling at his side and one arm extended in the air holding a stick with a small ball of fire on its end. The other arm holds a club.

Fear seized me: Oh Helion, why?

I look up. The huge club swiftly comes toward me; candlelight burns my eyes and

******

The pain in my head is such that I feel no other sensation. It is an immense, bludgeoning pain that throbs mostly in a swelling of considerable size. Uncomprehending this still, I reach back to rub the protrusion but the touch of my hand, light as it is, sends ever sharper stabs of pain through my whole construct.

I gasp, sucking in air until the pain subsides. For some time longer I lay in a myriad of feelings; I am nothing but feeling and they sway between consciousness and an aura of unconsciousness, then back again. Visions flood before me

    dim light
    bright
    brighter still the light and I
    i
who? why?
    Then total darkness.
    Eons passing.

    And rising from the dark again rising from dark again and again comes the small dim light again comes the light again again light like a pinpoint enters my eye then changes to flame wild fierce flame burning into countless transfigurations of
    stars
    stars and I flung among them and the woman, Selena Somewhere
    golden I am somewhere golden and silver flowers beside soft singing brooks
    again and again
    the bright
    the sun
    it is sun
       i
              am
                           sun.
Phoenixxxxxxxxx
through time
                    i

    I sense some small forms of continuity taking place within; my mind is close to full memory now.
    Them, but I am not of them. Yet I can no longer experience myself as Other than they. Where do I originate? Not among these. I am not here of my own volition.
    The, I am placed here.
    By whom?
    I AM NOT WHO I AM.

    I remember. But I remember so little of what I am remembering. What can a power mean? But Power is what my memory most holds of There. In me, I know that it was in me and I was It.
    But Here Now?
    "Eh", grunts one of them. There is a clang of chains; they return. My head aches tormentingly; my stomach is an awesome battlefield of harms and hurts I cannot yet understand. And besides these ills, compounded with what I now they call a-hunger, there comes a certain soreness around parts of my body. I recall a HereNow word, boils. Pestules. Tumors.
    I am completely body now and in the midst of my realiza-

tions, the door is smashed open and one of the beastlies enters. Auguring evil in its very appearance, it quickly crosses the dank cell floor and throws its booted foot into my groin. "Aiiieeeiii." I fall with the renewed pain and cry out in spite of myself.

What manner of creatures are these?

"Thar be wantin to see ya, now, vermin." It's concept was barely discernible, so he used another kick to convey comprehension, "Up, get!"

I forced myself up on one elbow; the entire cell swam around me like a sea, innundating around as the massive entity becomes a deep shaded shadow in the ensuing and encompassing darkness.

And even then, in my mind, light.

Why? How? What am I?

I grasp toward the outline of what appeared to be a stone but found it covered with slimy oozy surface that caused up to slip downward instead of rising. This, of course brought another blow from this most illogical of beings; for if he was so concerned that I rise, he should realize that his blows impede it. I fear they have no logic at all; even the elementary does not seem to penetrate the brain-thing in them.

He shouts again, "Up, ya here! And do it fast bastard, er the hounds'll have yere hide for poor fare."

Completely incomprehensible pronouncements. I consider reasoning with it, but what would be the use. In an odd sort of way it's very stupidity raises in me a feeling of protectiveness. The circle of circumstance that hold these creatures is unbending, and seemingly determined. I finally succeed, using all by bodily endowments to thrust myself to a standing position. On very faltering feet, I follow him.

He shoves me along a dark hallway, only dimly lit by flickering flames. I look away from the candlelight. I could not bare to see my memory of light turned to this. Perhaps it is because I have been so long in darkness that my eyes now see as they see. Perhaps not. For whatever reason, I begin to feel an enemity with light.

He shoves me down some stairs; I land at the bottom. There I'm dragged into a room crammed with spidery-looking devices, cranks, screws and all sort of bric-a-brac, none of which may be dignified with the name machinery, though seem somehow akin to what these beings will later called by that name.

Another kick from another creature. "Sweet Jesus!" I cry out, not fully knowing what I say, except that I sense a possibility of some curious mercy in their misrepresentation of enlightenment. But the name must have incensed, because it elicited another kick and the garbled question, "Be ye a wizard like thar's say ya be?"

"What? I can't distinguish the concept in your utterance."

"Arguu." It grunts with the force of the strength it is using as it kicks me again; my abdomen constricts. I am not able to control it and the bowel of the body try to empty, but as I have had not solid food, small strips of my intestines come forth in spots of blood.

I lay in the bilge, speaking weakly, seriously praying this time: "Merciful God, help me."

"Ha! Ya ha' th' courage to call on th' verra one ya blaspheme."

"What can you mean, sir? Surely you know there can be no irreverence in me. I ---"

Inexplicably these words elicited in him a feeling that I believe them to call "humanity". Consequently, this time without a blow, he asks, "Be ya wizard like Fawlks says? Be ye a practicer o' the black arts?"

Their magi; they believe me one of their magi. My mind floods with visions now: pyramids, sorceries, Mazda, of course. I am realizing that they are insatiable believers. In everything. A whole age of True Believers, though poor servants of the veracity they claim. They do in fact, come so close. That closeness has been a cause of concern among THEM west of Elion.

West of Elion?

Where do these names come from; these thoughts so strange to my HereNow? "Listen to me..." I begin, hoping he is an Initiate at the very least, "You see, there are realms of confusion in my mind at the moment. I'm not fully finished being constructed into your times so I cannot yet explain my complex confusion very well in word-term. But, in terms of valid relativity, and of course, what you conceive of as reality, what you sense as a curvature of time, which I need to tell you is in error, but nonetheless ..."

I was initially too involved in my explanation to note the horror that filled his eyes as I spoke; my words were only adding chaos to chaos. And yet, even when I did notice his reaction, I had some hope of explaining, and so continued: "Try to understand, you are so much more than you know. Begin by knowing I am one of THEM who would never harm you. You can understand, it is in you and it's not so difficult really. I am what you will be in time, you see. The thing is that you are clogged up with the faults and faiths of HereNow, now please don't get upset, I am not ridiculing your beliefs. No, no, because in truth, you have an inkling. It is there in your Initiates, in one who will use the cave allegory and so many more and most assuredly, you are most close in your visionaries, the Buddha, the Christos..."

"Holy Lord!" he gasped, made an awkward gesture around his head, stomach and shoulders and I experienced his emotions are tetter-tottering between fear and anger.

"Please. I know you believe it as Absolute Truth, and that's comprehensible based on the constructs of a millenium of..." I stopped mid-phrase: what could I possibly explain to them. More importantly, why was it so important to me, a need in me, to explain, "I am trying to tell you that there is much truth in what you believe. Take for example this idea of a Dark One, a Lucifer I think you call him. It is in truth, based on a real event in the eons, though that truth has been terribly garbled and misinterpreted by the tales that have arisen. In fact, there was an immortal who..."

"Immortal, ya say?"

"Yes, yes, well, in your terminology it's difficult for me to actually define the incorporation of vital entity structuralization that..."

His eye were two fires; he was no longer listening: "How come ya ta be in tha' cell?"

How could I explain that which I had not fully grasped: "That I cannot answer. Yet, I seem to have slipped through some form of Post-Continuum stratification that has rendered me..."

"No, no." He shouted for me to be silent, "Ya say na more ta me ya son o' Satan. The Holy Father'll be here and he'll be makin' shart work o' ya, I'll tell ya. Ya'll soon see yere Lucifer, I wager."

"But if you will only open your mind..."

"Bust open my head!" he kicked me, apparently finding a threat in my comment, "It be a Christian that put ya in the cell. That cell is never used, ya know that!"

"Never used?"

"Never. For no reason. It be locked shut tight forever, by

holy orders!"

"But why? Why locked this particular cell from use?" I blurted this, for herein surely was some clue to the link in the chain of my existence: "It's a well-built cell, is it not? All the other cells around it are in use. Why is it so singled out? It makes no sense. Perhaps you will explain some of the circumstances of how I came to be in there and that will help me unravel the mystery of my termporality here."

The new blow was his only means of expression. I felt in the swift tough of his hand, the swelter of incomprehensions that were his daily life; his meat of thought was lean indeed. That fact that this cell was always left unoccupied was but another inexplicable factor in a life filled with terrors, inconsistencies and an infinity of inexplicables. The acceptance, without question, of the unexplained was the science of these beastlies bowed beneath ignorance.

Then, as if bolted into, from outside him, his emotion changed, from anger, he began to tremble with fear, or perhaps, in them these are the same emotions. I soon saw the reason for this, for behind him, a large figure appeared on the far wall. I turned my gaze away from the omnious shadow to look at its source; I too trembled.

Cloaked all a-black, the fulsome hooded figure walks forward until it towers over my suffering body. The body is now filled to the brim of its fleshing encasement with every form of pain and illness capable in this entity-condition. A flickering candle makes a single shaft of light that seems to form an angry cross across the figure's face. I knew it was illusion, an appendage of my acquisition of their mentality only, but the impression was awesome. My previously brave inquisitor now knelt humbly before this new one, "Holy Father, it says words tha' ha no sense. He talks the language of the devil."

I lay in my own blood, puss oozing from the dozens of boils that dot my flesh. Intermittently, I cough up still more blood from the augy body; realizing without realizing: The Plague, too.

From the dark cavern of his cowl, a cavernous voice as black as its owner spoke to the kneeling man, "And you tell me, he was in the cell?"

"Ay, Father, in truth."

"No one would dare place a man there against Orders! No

one would have the courage to take this or any other into that forbidden place."

"I think no one did, good Father."

"And yet the deed was done."

"I cannot say how!" the man trembled, bowed his head.

"But you think he cast a spell on the jailer?"

"How else, Father?"

"No." I shouted protest. "No, it was not a spell. I only used Power to try to suspend his physical processes in order to obtain and substantiate the condition of his..." Once more I stopped in mid-phrase. More appropriate would be to say, that I was stopped, arrested in fact, by another curious event. The light of the candle had stopped flickering. In an instance, so brief that one could barely perceive it in normal temporal periods, the light was still for a near-second. Expectedly, the kneeling man did not perceive it. Unexpectedly, neither did the hooded dark one perceive.

Only I saw. That light; the quick, para-second when it was transfixed.

Beatific Vision; one of their phrases actually fit as a sharp crome orange beautiful face flashed before my sight and...

The flame flickered it away and once more the priest could be heard:

"Prepare him."

**

******

Some come and place my body on the rack.

Some put their hands out and turn screws and everywhere I feel in me every pain that has ever been inflicted on this species to which I have been condemned.

Some make the final vigorous twist and I feel body being torn asunder.

****

Barely conscious.

I twist again and again: Ah Yeus, Yeussssssss! I am shrieking.

A chorus of voices shout at me:

CONFESS!!! CONFESS!!! SPEAK, BLASPHEMER!!!

ADMIT YOUR WIZARDRY!!!

DEVIL YOU ARE!!!

ADMIT YOU CAUSE THE PLAGUE!!!

CONFESS!!! CONFESS!!!

"I confess." I mutter.

Some come down and take me through a long winding staircase.

My ruined body falls to and fro until I fall out of the cart.

Some come and take my arms; I am lifted away again. I wince at the rough grasp that tears more of my skin away. The boils burst and puss oozes; I am caked with the mire and ills of Body.

I am dragged down cobbled streets; my body is bounced over other dead bodies of the people, dogs and beasts on the street where the crude wagon takes me.

Frogs and vermin lie strewn upon the bleeding plague-heap of dead and dying humanity.

And even now, I pity them.

I cry out against the gods that create these limited creatures of a day

why, why create these unintended lives with all their attendent ills and then leave them to themselves; lone specks in a dazzling shining universe that---

Others come; the few remaining living and they gather twigs and wood and they sing hymns of hatred:

burn burn burn

burn burn burn burn burn

   Oh, burn burn burn burn,

      good Lord, burn burn burn

Fragments are ripped from my flesh; what is left of me is thrown up on a platform. I am thrust up and stakes hold me to a pole in the center. More wood and twigs are piled around me

Some come and put fire there to light my death

I am to die.

I?

Who am I to die?

I will die without knowing; knowledge is the only possible redemption I can

Hope, and I will not have it.

Did I even have life? A place? Have I lived? I who am about to die: did I live?

Flames flare. Flames leap upward; up the ankles, up thighs, the stomach, my chest, I am a fiery state, I am consumed.
I gaze into burning light.

Mesmerized my eyes turn to gold coals: I am seared who cry out, "No more, O Helion, no more!"

****

Clear bright luminosity.
Shivery shimming shining lights:

Ah, I am returning: Lord of Many Names am I: I am Aether: I am Phosphor; I am Hesper
I am Aurora
I am Hyperion
I am Phoebus, Phoenix, and

I flash upward upward like a sun through Sirius, I wind west of Saiph and over Orion, I go beyond Bellatrix as I flash, I go as light and I play along the Pleiacles
Body no longer, I know not even a dream of dark, no here, no now, I am Lord of Bright Spaces, soaring as I swirl in flashflesh around Capella and Auriga, toward Castor and Pollox
    I swirl   I am shining
I sparkle as I soar to Brethren; I sink in purelight: O Helion, Father, I return among the Circles of Light and I stand in your center. I hear, you are speaking:
'THOU, LORD OF BRIGHT SPACES; THOU, LORD OF MANY NAMES,
THOUGH PROMETHEUS, THOU LUCIFER EVERY PITYING THE DARKLINGS
BEYOND ELION: THOU WHO WOULD GIVE THEM THE FIRE
AND KNOWING THAT WILL LEAD TO THE IMPOSSIBLE ASPIRING
THAT WILL ALLOW THEM TO THINK OF THEMSELVES AS BEYOND
THEIR LIMITATIONS
THINK OF THEMSELVES

AS WE,

SO WE, CONDEMN YOU FOREVER TO – – – –

****

Over the river a dark dank fog spreads upward.
It is the year 1347, Annos Domini.

The fog hovers.
Then the fog begins to spread itself as if it is guided by some other intelligence; as if it is moving in accordance with some clear predestined Intent.
The fog meanders in dark shadows crawling up passed Gray Mond's Cathedral; passed the pillories. The fog moves like a silent song along the drawbridge. It stops. It scans the moat of the castle and then slowly climbs up the castle wall and enters it like a cold deathgas.
Through the stone crevices, down the dim halls and into the cell, the fog.
Every night now: This same dream.

Dedication: to the sisters: sources of much of my fiction and not a
little, of my reality.
To Mary Green, and our "upper unholy trinity"
Angeline Footo
Melly Woolwine, and
Kathrine Price

Thanks, Jean